Locus Elm Press

presents

WILLIAM LAZENBY'S

The Pearl

A JOURNAL OF FACETIÆ AND VOLUPTUOUS READING

VOLUMES I to IV

LOCUS ELM™

also published by

Locus Elm Press

Erotica at:

Amazon United Kingdom

Amazon United States of America

Amazon Germany

Amazon Netherlands

Amazon France

Amazon Spain

Amazon Canada

Amazon Australia

Amazon Brazil

Amazon Japan

Amazon Mexico

Amazon Italy

Amazon India

* * *

on Nook at:

Barnes & Noble

* * *

for Kobo at:

Kobo Store

* * *

and on Google Books at:

Google Play Store

The Pearl

A Journal of Facetiæ and Voluptuous Reading

VOLUMES I to IV

by
Anonymous

written 1879

Originally published by William Lazenby in 1879 being the precursor to the
Victorian erotic periodicals *The Oyster* and *The Boudoir.*

This paperback edition - Copyright: Locus Elm Press

Published: July 2015

TABLE OF CONTENTS

VOLUME I

* * * * *

Published Monthly

July. 1879

AN APOLOGY FOR OUR TITLE

Having decided to bring out a Journal, the Editor racks his brains for a suitable name with which to christen his periodical. Friends are generally useless in an emergency of this kind; they suggest all kinds of impossible names; the following were some of the titles proposed in this instance: "Facts and Fancies," "The Cremorne," "The All Round," "The Monthly Courses," "The Devil's Own," and "Dugdale's Ghost"; The two first had certainly great attractions to our mind, but at last our own ideas have hit upon the modest little "Pearl," as more suitable, especially in the hope that when it comes under the snouts of the moral and hypocritical swine of the world, they may not trample it underfoot, and feel disposed to rend the publisher, but that a few will become subscribers on the quiet. To such better disposed piggywiggys, I would say, for encouragement, that they have only to keep up appearances by regularly attending church, giving to charities, and always appearing deeply interested in moral philanthropy, to ensure a respectable and highly moral character, and that if they only are clever enough never to be found out, they may, sub rosa, study and enjoy the philosophy of life till the end of their days, and earn a glorious and saintly epitaph on their tombstone, when at last the Devil pegs them out.

EDITOR OF THE "PEARL"

SUB-UMBRA, OR SPORT AMONG THE SHE-NOODLES

The merry month of May has always been famous for its propitious influence over the voluptuous senses of the fairer sex.

I will tell you two or three little incidents which occurred to me in May, 1878, when I went to visit my cousins in Sussex, or as I familiarly call them, the She-Noodles, for the sport they afforded me at various times.

My uncle's is a nice country residence, standing in large grounds of its own, and surrounded by small fields of arable and pasture land, interspersed by numerous interesting copses, through which run footpaths and shady walks, where you are not likely to meet anyone in a month. I shall not trouble my readers with the name of the locality, or they may go pleasure hunting for themselves. Well, to go on, these cousins consisted of Annie, Sophie, and Polly, beside their brother Frank, who, at nineteen, was the eldest, the girls being younger. After dinner, the first day of my arrival, paterfamilias and mamma both indulged in a snooze in their armchair, whilst us boys and girls (I was the same age as Frank) took a stroll in the grounds. I attached myself more particularly to cousin Annie, a finely developed blonde, with deep blue eyes, pouting red lips, and a full heaving bosom, which to me looked like a perfect volcano of smothered desires. Frank was a very indolent fellow, who loved to smoke his cigar, and expected his sisters, who adored him, to sit by his side, reading some of the novels of the day, or tell him their love secrets, &c. This was by far too tame an amusement for me, and as I had not been there for nearly three years, I requested Annie to show me the improvements in the grounds before we went in to tea, saying to Frank, banteringly, "I suppose, old fellow, you're too, lazy, and would prefer your sister taking me round?"

"I'm too comfortable; lazy is an ugly word, Walter, but the fact is, Soph is just reading a most interesting book, and I can't leave it," he replied; "besides, sissie is quite as well, or better qualified than I am to show off the grounds. I never notice anything."

"Come on, Annie," said I taking her hand; "Frank is in love."

"No, I'm sure he never thinks of a girl, except his sisters," was the reply.

We were now out of earshot, in a shady walk, so I went on a little more freely. "But, surely you, coz, are in love, if he is not. I can tell it by your liquid eye and heaving bosom."

A scarlet flush shot over her features at my allusion to her finely moulded bosom, but it was evidently pleasing, and far from offensive, to judge by her playfully spoken, "Oh! Walter, for shame, sir!"

We were a good distance away by this time, and a convenient seat stood near, so throwing my arms around the blushing girl, I kissed her ruby lips, and drawing her with me, said, "Now, Annie, dear, I'm your cousin and old playfellow, I couldn't help kissing those beautiful lips, which I might always make free with when we were little boy and girl together; now you shall confess all before I let you go."

"But I've nothing to confess, sir."

"Do you never think of love, Annie? Look me in the face if you can say it's a stranger to your bosom," putting my hand familiarly round her neck till my right hand rested on one of the panting globes of her bosom.

She turned her face to mine, suffused as it was by a deeper blush than ever, as her dark blue eyes met mine, in a fearless search of my meaning, but instead of speaking in response to this mute appeal, I kissed her rapturously, sucking in the fragrance of her sweet breath till she fairly trembled with emotion.

It was just beginning to get dusk, my hands were caressing the white, firm flesh of her beautiful neck, slowly working their way towards the heaving bubbies a little lower down; at last I whispered, "What a fine, what a lovely bust you have developed since I saw you last, dear Annie, you won't mind your cousin, will you, when everything used to be so free to each other; besides, what harm can there be in it?"

She seemed on fire, a thrill of emotion seemed to shoot through both of us, and for several moments she lay almost motionless in my arms, with one hand resting on my thigh. Priapus was awake and ready for business, but she suddenly aroused herself, saying, "We must never stop here, let us walk round or they will suspect something."

"When shall we be alone again, darling? We must arrange that before we go in," I said quickly.

It was impossible to keep her on the seat, but as we walked on she said, musingly, "To-morrow morning we might go for a stroll before lunch, Frank lies in bed, and my sisters are keeping house this week; I shall have to mind the tarts and pies next week."

I gave her another hug and a kiss, as I said, "How delightful that will be; what a dear, thoughtful girl you are, Annie."

"Mind, sir, how you behave to-morrow, not so much kissing, or I shan't take you for a second walk; here we are at the house."

Next morning was gloriously warm and fine; as soon as breakfast was over we started for our stroll, being particularly minded by papa to be back in good time for luncheon.

I gradually drew out my beautiful cousin, till our conversation got exceedingly warm, the hot blood rushing in waves of crimson over her shamefaced visage.

"What a rude boy you have grown Walter, since you were here last; I can't help blushing at the way you run on, sir!" she exclaimed at last.

"Annie, my darling," I replied, "what can be more pleasing than to talk of fun with pretty girls, the beauties of their legs and bosoms, and all about them? How I should love to see your lovely calf at this moment, especially after the glimpses I have already had of a divine ankle," saying which I threw myself under a shady tree, close by a gate in a meadow, and drew the half-resisting girl down on the grass at my side, and kissed her passionately, as I murmured, "Oh! Annie, what is there worth living for like the sweets of love?"

Her lips met mine in a fiery embrace, but suddenly disengaging herself, her eyes cast down, and looking awfully abashed, she stammered out, "What is it? what do you mean, Walter?"

"Ah, coz dear, can you be so innocent? Feel here the dart of love all impatient to enter the mossy grotto between your thighs," I whispered, placing her hand upon my prick, which I had suddenly let out of the restraining trousers. "How you sigh; grasp it in your hand, dear, is it possible that you do not understand what it is for?"

Her face was crimson to the roots of her hair, as her hand grasped my tool, and her eyes seemed to start with terror at the sudden apparition of Mr. John Thomas; so that taking advantage of her speechless confusion my own hand, slipping under her clothes, soon had possession of her mount, and in spite of the nervous contraction of her thighs, the forefinger searched out the virgin clitoris.

"Ah! oh! oh!! Walter don't; what are you about?"

"It's all love, dear, open your thighs a wee bit and see what pleasure my finger will make you experience," I again whispered, smothering her with renewed and luscious kisses, thrusting the velvet tip of my tongue between her lips.

"Oh! oh! you will hurt!" she seemed to sigh rather than speak, as her legs relaxed a little of their spasmodic contraction.

My lips continued glued to hers, our otherwise disengaged arms clasped each other closely round the waist, her hand holding my affair in a kind of convulsive grasp, whilst my fingers were busy with clitoris and cunny; the only audible sound resembling a mixture of kisses and sighs, till all in a moment I felt her crack deluged with a warm, creamy spend whilst my own juice spurted over her hand and dress in loving sympathy.

In a short while we recovered our composure a little, and I then explained to her that the melting ecstasy she had just felt was only a slight foretaste of the joy I could give her, by inserting my member in her cunny. My persuasive eloquence and the warmth of her desires soon overcame all maiden fears and scruples; then for fear of damaging her dress, or getting the green stain of the grass on the knees of my light trousers, I persuaded her to stand up by the gate and allow me to enter behind. She hid her face in her hands on the top rail of the gate, as I slowly raised her dress; what glories were unfolded to view, my prick's stiffness was renewed in an instant at the sight of her delicious buttocks, so beautifully relieved by the white of her pretty drawers; as I opened them and exposed the flesh, I could see the lips of her plump pouting cunny, deliciously feathered, with soft light down, her lovely legs, drawers, stockings, pretty boots, making a tout ensemble, which as I write and describe them cause Mr. Priapus to swell in my breeches; it was a most delicious sight.

I knelt and kissed her bottom, slit, and everything my tongue could reach, it was all mine, I stood up and prepared to take possession of the seat of love -- when, alas! a sudden shriek from Annie, her clothes dropped, all my arrangements were upset in a moment; a bull had unexpectedly appeared on the opposite side of the gate, and frightened my love by the sudden application of his cold, damp nose to her forehead. It is too much to contemplate that scene even now.

(To be continued.)

MISS COOTE'S CONFESSION, OR THE VOLUPTUOUS EXPERIENCES OF AN OLD MAID

In a series of Letters to a Lady Friend.

*

Letter I

My Dear Girl,

I know I have long promised you an account of the reason of my penchant for the rod, which, in my estimation, is one of the most voluptuous and delicious institutions of private life, especially to a supposed highly respectable old maid like your esteemed friend. Treaties must be carried out, and promises kept, or how can I ever hope for the pleasure of making you taste my little green tickler again. Writing, and especially a sort of confession of my voluptuous weakness, is a most unpleasant task, as I feel as shamefaced in putting these things on paper as when my grandfather's housekeeper first bared my poor blushing little bottom to his ruthless attack. My only consolation at commencing is the hope that I shall warm to the subject as it progresses, in my endeavour to depict, for your gratification, some of the luscious episodes of my early days.

My grandfather, as you well know, was the celebrated Indian General, Sir Eyre Coote, almost as well known for his eight-penny fiasco with the Bluecoat boys as for his services to the Hon. E. I. Company. He was a confirmed martinet, and nothing delighted him so much as a good opportunity for the use of the cat, but I cannot tell you anything about that, as that was before my time.

My first recollection of hint is after the aforesaid City scandal, when he had to retire from public life in comparative disgrace. My parents both died when I was just a lad, and the old General, who had no other relatives to care for, took entire charge of me, and, at his death, I was left his sole heiress, and mistress of nearly £3,000 per annum.

He resided in a quiet country house some twenty miles from London, where I spent the first few months of my orphaned life, with only his housekeeper, Mrs. Mansell, and the two servants, Jane and Jemima. The old General being away in Holland searching, so I afterwards heard, for original editions respecting the practices of Cornelius Hadrien, a curious work on the flagellation of religious penitents by a father confessor.

It was the middle of summer when he returned, and I soon found the liberty I had been enjoying considerably restricted. Orders not to pluck the flowers, or the fruit in the garden; and a regular lesson set me every day by the old autocrat himself. At first they were tolerably simple, but gradually increased in difficulty, and now, in after years, I can plainly understand his wolf and lamb tactics, by which I must eventually fall under his assumed just displeasure.

What gave me considerable pleasure at this time was his decided objection to mourning, or anything at all sombre in my dress. He said my parents had been shown every possible respect by wearing black for months, and I must now be dressed as became a young lady of my good expectations.

Although we scarcely ever received company, and then only some old fogy of his military acquaintance, I was provided with a profusion of new and elegant dresses, as well as beautiful shoes, slippers, drawers, and underlinen, all trimmed with finest lace &c., not even forgetting some very beautiful garters, a pair of which with gold buckles, he would insist upon putting on for me, taking no notice of my blushing confusion, as he pretended to arrange my drawers and skirts afterwards, but merely to remark: What a fine figure I should make, if they ever had to strip me for punishment.

Soon my lessons began to be harder than I could fairly manage. One day he expostulated, "Oh! Rosa; Rosa!! why don't you try to be a better girl. I don't want to punish you."

"But grandfather," I replied, "how can I learn so much of that horrid French every day. I'm sure no one else could do it."

"Hold your tongue, Miss Pert, I must be a better judge than a little girl like you."

"But, grandfather dear, you know I do love you, and I do try my best."

"Well, prove your love and diligence in future, or your posterior must feel a nice little birch, I shall get ready for you," said he sternly.

Another week passed, during which I could not help observing an unusual fire and sparkle in his eyes, whenever I appeared in evening dress at the dinner table (we always dined in quiet state), and he also suggested that I ought to wear a choice little bouquet of fresh flowers in my bosom, to set off my complexion.

But the climax was approaching, I was not to escape long; he again found fault, and gave me what he gravely called one last chance: my eyes were filled with tears, and I trembled to look at his stern old face, and knew any remonstrance on my part would be useless.

The prospect of punishment made me so nervous, it was with the greatest difficulty I could attend to my lessons, and the second day after, I broke down entirely.

"Oh! Ho! it's come to this has it, Rosie?" said the old gentleman, "nothing will do, you must be punished."

Ringing the bell for Mrs. Mansell, he told her to have the punishment room and the servants all ready, when he should want them, as he was sorry to say "Miss Rosa was so idle, and getting worse and worse with her lessons every day, she must now be taken severely in hand or she would be spoiled for life."

"Now, you bad girl," said he, as the housekeeper retired, "go to your room and reflect upon what your idleness has brought to you."

Full of indignation, confusion, and shame, I rushed to my chamber, and bolted the door, determined they should break the door down first before I would submit to such a public exposure, before the two servants; throwing myself on the bed, I gave vent to my tears for at least a couple of hours, expecting every moment the dreadful summons to attend the old man's punishment drill, as he called it, but, no one disturbing me, I at last came to the conclusion it was only a plan of his to frighten me, and so I fell into a soothing sleep. A voice at the door awakened me, and I recognized the voice of Jane, as she said, "Miss Rosa, Miss Rosa, you'll be late for dinner."

"No dinner for me, Jane, if I'm going to be punished; go away, leave me alone," whispered I through the keyhole.

"Oh! Miss Rosie, the General's been in the garden all the afternoon, quite good-tempered, perhaps he's forgotten it all; don't make him angry by not being ready for dinner, let me in quick."

So I cautiously drew the bolt, and let her assist me to dress.

"Cheer up, Miss Rosie, don't look dull, go down as if nothing had happened, and most likely all will be forgotten; his memory is so short, especially if you put in your bosom this sweet little nosegay to please him, as you have never done it since he said it would set off your complexion."

Thus encouraged, I met my grandfather with a good appetite, and, as if the "bitterness was past," like Agag before Samuel, little suspecting I should be almost hewed in pieces afterwards.

The dinner passed most pleasantly, for such a formal affair as my grandfather made it, he took several glasses of wine, and in the middle of the dessert seemed to contemplate me with unusual interest; at last suddenly seeming to notice the little bouquet of damask and white roses, he said, "That's right, Rosa, I see you have carried out my suggestion of a nosegay at last; it quite improves your appearance, but nothing to what my birch will effect on your naughty bottom, which will soon look like one of those fine peaches, and now's the time to do it," said he, ringing the bell.

Almost distracted, and ready to faint, I rushed for the door, but only in time to fall into the arms of strong Jemima.

"Now for punishment drill; march on, Jemima, with the culprit, you've got her safe; Mrs. Mansell and Jane, come on," said he to them, as they appeared in the background.

Resistance was useless. I was soon carried into a spare room I had never entered; it contained very little furniture, except the carpet, and one comfortable easy chair; but on the walls hung several bunches of twigs, and in one corner stood a thing like a stepladder, but covered with red baize, and fitted with six rings, two halfway up, two at bottom, and two at the top.

"Tie her to the horse, and get ready for business," said the General, as he seated himself in the chair, to look on at his ease.

"Come, Rosa, dear, don't be troublesome, and make your grandfather more angry," said Mrs. Mansell, unfastening my waistband. "Slip off your dress, whilst the girls put the horse in the middle of the room."

"Oh! No! No! I won't be whipped," I screamed. "Oh! Sir! Oh! Grandfather, do have mercy," said I, throwing myself on my knees before the old man.

"Come, come, it's no use showing the white feather, Rosa, it's for your own good. No more nonsense. Mrs. Mansell, do your duty, and let us get the painful business over; she isn't one of my stock if she doesn't show her pluck when it comes to the pinch."

The three women all tried to lift me, but I kicked, scratched, and bit all round, and, for a moment or two, almost beat them off in my fury, but my strength was soon exhausted, and Jemima, smarting from a severe bite, carried me in vengeful triumph to the dreaded machine. Quick as thought, my hands and feet were secured to the upper and lower rings; the horse widening towards the ground caused my legs to be well apart when drawn up closely to the rings at my ankles.

I could hear Sir Eyre chuckle with delight, as he exclaimed, "By God! she's a vixen, and it must be taken out of her, she's a Coote all over. Bravo, Rosie! Now get her ready quickly."

I submitted in sullen despair, whilst my torn dress and underskirts were turned up and pinned round my shoulders, but when they began to unloose my drawers, my rage burst out afresh, and turning my head, I saw the old man, his stern face beaming with pleased animation, whisking in his right hand a small bunch of fresh birchen twigs. My blood was in a boil, and my bottom tingled with anticipated strokes, especially when Jemima, pulling the drawers nearly down to my knees, gave me a smart little slap on the sly, to let me know what I might soon expect, and I fairly shouted, "You must be a cruel old beast to let them treat me so."

"Old beast, indeed!" said he, jumping up in a passion. "We'll see about that, Miss; perhaps you'll be glad to apologize before long."

I saw him stepping forward. "Oh! Mercy! Mercy! Sir! I didn't mean it; they've hurt me so; I couldn't help what I said."

"This is a really serious case," said he, apparently addressing the others. "She's idle, violently vicious, and even insulting to me, her only natural guardian, instead of treating me with proper respect. There can be no alternative, the only remedy, however painful the scene may be to us who have to inflict the punishment, is to carry it out, as a matter of duty, or the girl will be ruined. She has never been under proper control all her life."

"Oh! Grandfather, punish me any way but this. I know I can't bear it; it's so dreadfully cruel," I sobbed out through my tears,

"My child, such crocodile tears have no effect on me; you must be made to feel the smart. If we let you off now, you would be laughing at it all, and go on worse than before. Stand aside, Jane, we can't waste any more time." So saying, he made a flourish with the rod, so as to make quite an audible "whisk" in the air. I suppose it was only to clear the way, as it did not touch me; in fact up to this time, he had treated me like a cat which knows the poor mousey cannot escape, but may be pounced upon at any time.

I could see the tears in Jane's eyes, but Jemima had a malicious smile on her face, and Mrs. Mansell looked very grave, but no time was allowed for reflections; the next instant I felt a smart but not heavy stroke right across my loins, then another, and another, in rather quick succession, but not too fast for me to think that perhaps after all it would not be so dreadful as I feared; so setting my teeth firmly without uttering a word, I determined to give as little indication as possible of my feelings. All this and a great deal more flashed through my brain before six strokes had been administered, my bottom tingled all over, and the blood seemed to rush like lightning through my veins at every blow, and my face felt as my poor posteriors.

"Now, you idle puss," said the General, "you begin to feel the fruits of your conduct. Will you? Will you call me an old beast again?" giving a harder stroke at each ejaculation.

My courage still sustained my resolution not to cry out, but only seemed to make him more angry.

"Sulky tempered and obstinate, by Jove!" he continued; "we must draw it out of you. Don't think, Miss, I'm to be beaten by a little wench like you; take that, and that, and that," whisking me with still greater energy, concluding with a tremendous whack which drew up the skin to bursting tension, and I felt another like it would make the blood spurt forth, but he suddenly paused in his fury, as if for want of breath, but as I now know too well, only to prolong his own exquisite pleasure.

Thinking all was over, I entreated them to let me go, but to my sorrow soon found my mistake.

"Not yet, not yet, you bad girl, you're not half punished for all your biting, scratching, and impudence," exclaimed Sir Eyre.

Again the hateful birch hissed through the air, and cut into my bruised flesh, both buttocks and thighs, suffering and smarting in agony, but he seemed careful at first not to draw the blood; however, I was not to escape, it was only his deliberate plan of attack, so as not to exhaust the poor victim too soon.

"Bite, and scratch, and fight against my orders again, will you? Miss Rosie, you'll know next time what to expect. You deserve no mercy, the idleness was bad enough, but such murderous conduct is awful; I believe you would have killed anyone in your passion if you could. Bite, scratch, and fight, eh! Bite, will you?" Thus lectured the old man, getting warmer and warmer in his attack, till the blood fairly trickled down my poor thighs.

I was in dreadful agony at every cut, and must have fainted, but his lecturing seemed to sustain me like a cordial; besides, with the pain I experienced a most pleasurable warmth and excitability impossible to be described, but which, doubtless, you, my dear, have felt for yourself when under my discipline.

But all my fortitude could not much longer suppress my sighs and moans, and at last I felt as if I must die under the torture, in spite of the exquisite sensation which mingled with it; notwithstanding my ohs and ahs, and stifled cries, I would not ask for mercy again; my sole thoughts ran upon the desire for vengeance, and how I should like to whip and cut them all in pieces, especially the General and Jemima, and even poor tearful Jane, Sir Eyre seemed to forget his age, and worked away in frightful excitement.

"Damme, won't you cry for mercy? Won't you apologize, you young hussy," he hissed between his teeth. "She's tougher and more obstinate than any of the family, a real chip of the old block. But to be beaten by the young spitfire, Mrs. Mansell, is more than I can bear. There! there! there!" cried he; and at last the worn-out stump of the rod fell from his hand, as he sank back quite exhausted in his chair.

"Mrs. Mansell," he gasped, "give her half-a-dozen good stripes with a new rod to finish her off, and let her know that although she may exhaust an old man, there are other strong arms that can dispense justice to her impudent rump."

The housekeeper, in obedience to the command, takes up a fine fresh birch, and cuts deliberately, counting, in clear voice, one, two, three, four, five, six (her blows were heavy, but did not seem to sting so cruelly as those given by Sir Eyre). "There," she says, "Miss Rosa, I might have laid it on more heavily, but I pitied you this first time."

Nearly dead, and frightfully cut up, although victorious, I had to be carried to my room. But what a victory? all torn and bleeding, as I was, besides the certainty that the old General would renew his attack the first favourable opportunity.

Poor Jane laughed and cried over my lacerated posteriors as she tenderly washed me with cold arnica and water, and she seemed so used to the business that when we retired to rest (for I got her to sleep with me) I asked her if she had not often attended bruised bottoms before,

"Yes, Miss Rosie," she replied; "but you must keep the secret and not pretend to know anything. I have been whipped myself, but not so bad as you were, although it's cruel. We all rather like it after the first time or two; especially if we are not cut up too much. Next time you should shout out well for mercy, &c., as it pleases the old man, and he won't be so furious. He was so bad and exhausted with whipping you, Mrs. Mansell was going to send for the doctor, but Jemima said a good birching would do him more good, and draw the blood away from his head; so they pickled him finely, till he quite came to himself, and begged hard to be let off."

Thus ended my first lesson; and, in further letters, you shall hear how I got on with Jane, continued the contest with the General, my adventures at Mrs. Flaybum's school, and my own domestic discipline since left to myself.

Believe me, Dear Nellie, Your affectionate friend, Rosa Belinda Coote.

(To be continued)

LADY POKINGHAM; OR THEY ALL DO IT

Giving an Account of her Luxurious Adventures, both before and after her Marriage with Lord Crim-Con

*

Introduction

To the Reader,

Very little apology will be needed for putting in print the following highly erotic and racy narrative of a young patrician lady, whose adventures I feel assured every genuine lover of voluptuous reading will derive as much or more pleasure afforded your humble servant,

The subject of these memoirs was one of the brightest and most charming of her sex, endued with such exquisite nervous sensitiveness, in addition to an unusual warmth of constitution that she was quite unable to resist the seductive influences of God's finest creation; for God made man in his own image, male and female, created he them; and this was the first commandment, "Be faithful and multiply, and replenish the earth"--see Genesis, chapter 1.

The natural instinct of the ancients instilled in their minds the idea that copulation was the direct and most acceptable form of worship they could offer to their deities, and I know that those of my readers who are not bigoted Christians will agree with me, that there cannot be any great sin in giving way to natural desires, and enjoying, to the utmost, all those delicious sensations for which a beneficent Creator has so amply fitted us.

Poor girl, she did not live long, and in thoroughly enjoying her few briefs years of butterfly life, who can think her wicked!

The scraps from which my narrative is compiled were found in a packet she had entrusted to a devoted servitor, who, after her sudden and premature death at the early age of twenty-three, entered my service.

As author, I feel the crudeness of my style may be a little offensive to some, but hope my desire to afford general pleasure will excuse my defects.

THE AUTHOR.

Part I

My dear Walter,

How I love you! but alas! you will never know it till I am gone; little do you think, as you wheel me about in my invalid chair, how your delicate attentions have won the heart of a poor consumptive on the verge of the grave. How I long to suck the sweets of love from your lips; to fondle and caress your lordly priapus, and feel its thrilling motions within me; but such joys cannot be, the least excitement would be my death, and I can but sigh as I look at your kind loving face, and admire the fine proportions of my darling, as evidenced by the large bunch of keys you always seem to have in your pocket; indeed you look to have a key of keys, whose burning thrusts would unlock any virgin cabinet.

This is a strange fancy of mine (the writing for your perusal a short account of some of my adventures); but one of the only pleasures left me is to indulge in reveries of the past, and seem to feel over again the thrilling emotions of voluptuous enjoyments, which are now denied to me; and I hope the recital of my escapades and follies may afford you some slight pleasure, and add to the lasting regard with which I hope you will remember me in years to come. One thing I ask of you, dear Walter, is to fancy you are enjoying Beatrice Pokingham when you are in the embraces of some future inamorata. It is a pleasure I have often indulged in myself when in the action of coition, and heightened my bliss by letting my fancy run riot, and imagined I was in the arms of someone I particularly wished for, but could not come at. My income dies with me, so I have no cause to make a will, but you will find notes for a few hundred pounds enclosed with this outline of my adventures, which is all I have been able to save.

You will also find a fine lock of dark brown hair, which I have cut from the abundant chevelure of my Mons Veneris; other friends and relatives may have the admired curls from my head, your memento is cut from the sacred spot of love.

I never remember my father, the Marquis of Pokingham, but have my doubts as to whether I am really entitled to the honour of claiming him as a parent, as he was a used-up old , man, and from papers and letters, which passed privately between him and my mother, I know that he more than suspected he was indebted to his good-looking footman for the pretty baby girl my mother presented to him; as he says in one note, "that he could have forgiven everything if the fruits of her intercourse with James had been a son and heir, so as to keep his hated nephew out of the estates and title, and wished her to let him cultivate her parsley bed for another crop, which might perhaps turn out more in accordance with his wishes." The poor old fellow died soon after writing that note, and my mother, from whom this dreadful consumption is transmitted to me, also left me an orphan at an early age, leaving me her jointure of £20,000, and an aristocratic title which that amount was quite inadequate to properly support.

My guardians were very saving and careful, as they sent me to school young, and only spent about £150 a year for schooling and necessaries, till they thought it was time for me to be brought out in the world, so that I benefitted considerably by the accumulated interest of my money.

The first four years of my school passed away uneventfully, and during that time I was only in one serious scrape, which 1 will relate, as it led to my first taste of a good birch rod.

Miss Birch was rather an indulgent schoolmistress, and only had to resort to personal punishment for very serious offenses, which she considered might materially affect the future character of her pupils, unless thoroughly cut out of them from the first. I had a sudden fancy for making sketches on my slate in school. One of our governesses, Miss Pennington, was a rather crabbed and severe old girl of five-

and-thirty, and particularly evoked my abilities as a caricaturist, and the sketches would be slyly passed from one to the other of us, causing considerable giggling and gross inattention to our lessons. I was infatuated and conceited with what I considered my clever drawings and several admonitions and extra tasks as punishment had no effect in checking my mischievous interruptions, until one afternoon Miss Birch had fallen asleep at her desk, and old Penn was busy with a class, when the sudden inspiration seized me to make a couple of very rude sketches; one of the old girl sitting on a chamber utensil; but the other was a rural idea of her stooping down, with her clothes up to ease herself, in a field. The first girl I showed them to almost burst with laughter, and two others were so anxious to see the cause of her mirth, that they were actually stooping over her shoulder to look at my slate, when, before I could possibly get to it to rub them off, old Penn pounced upon it like an eagle, and carried it in triumph to Miss Birch, who was awakened chagrined by the amused smile which our principal could not repress at first sight of the indecent caricatures.

"My young lady must smart for this, Miss Pennington," said Miss Birch, with suddenly assumed gravity; "she has been very troublesome lately with these impudent drawings, but this is positively obscene; if she draws one thing she will go to another. Send for Susan to bring my birch rod! I must punish her whilst my blood is warm, as I am too forgiving, and may let her off."

I threw myself on my knees, and implored for mercy, promising "Never, never to do anything of the kind again."

Miss Birch.-"You should have thought of the consequences before you drew such filthy pictures; the very idea of one of my young ladies being capable of such productions is horrible to me; these prurient ideas cannot be allowed to settle in your mind for an instant, if I can whip them out."

Miss Pennnington, with a grim look of satisfaction, now took me by the wrist, just as Susan, a stout, strong, fair servant girl of about twenty, appeared with what looked to me a fearful big bunch of birch twigs, neatly tied up with red velvet ribbon.

"Now, Lady Beatrice Pokingham," said Miss Birch, "kneel down, confess your fault, and kiss the rod," taking the bunch from Susan's hands, and extending it to me as a queen might her sceptre to a supplicant subject.

Anxious to get over the inevitable, and make my punishment as light as possible, I knelt down, and with real tears of penitence begged her to be as lenient as her sense of justice would admit, as I knew I well deserved what she was going to inflict, and would take care not to insult Miss Pennington again, whom I was very sorry to have so caricatured; then I kissed the rod and resigned myself to my fate.

Miss Pennington, maliciously.-"Ah! Miss Birch, how quickly the sight of the rod makes hypocritical repentance."

Miss Birch.-"I quite understand all that, Miss Pennington, but must temper justice with mercy at the proper time; now, you impudent artist, lift your clothes behind, and expose your own bottom to the justly merited punishment."

With trembling hands I lifted my skirts, and was then ordered to open my drawers also; which done, they pinned up my dress and petticoats as high as my shoulders; then I was laid across a desk, and Susan stood in front of me, holding both hands, whilst old Penn and the French governess (who had just entered the schoolroom) each held one of my legs, so that I was what you might call helplessly spread-eagled.

Miss Birch, looking seriously round as she flourished the rod.-"Now, all you young ladies, let this whipping be a caution to you; my Lady Beatrice richly deserves this degrading shame, for her indecent (I ought to call them obscure) sketches. Will you! will you, you troublesome, impudent little thing, ever do so again? There, there, there, I hope it will soon do you good. Ah! you may scream; there's a few more to come yet."

The bunch of birch seemed to crash on my bare bottom with awful force; the tender skin smarted, and seemed ready to burst at every fresh cut. "Ah! ah! oh!!! Oh, heavens! have mercy, madame. Oh! I will never do anything like it again. Ah-r-re! I can't bear it!" I screamed, kicking and struggling under every blow, so that at first they could scarcely hold me, but I was soon exhausted by my own efforts.

Miss Birch,-"You can feel it a little, may it do you good, you bad little girl; if I don't check you now, the whole establishment would soon be demoralized. Ah! ha! your bottom is getting finely wealed, but I haven't done yet," cutting away with increasing fury.

Just then I caught a glimpse of her face, which was usually pale, but now flushed with excitement, and her eyes sparkled with unwonted animation. "Ah!" she continued, "young ladies beware of my rod, when I do have to use it. How do you like it, Lady Beatrice? Let us all know how nice it is," cutting my bottom and thighs deliberately at each ejaculation.

Lady Beatrice.-"Ah! oh! ah-r-r-re! It's awful! Oh I shall die if you don't have mercy, Miss Birch. Oh! my God, I'm fearfully punished; I'm cut to pieces; the birch feels as if it was red hot, the blows burn so!"

Then I felt as if it was all over, and I must die soon; my cries were succeeded by low sobs, moans, and then hysterical crying, which gradually got lower and lower, till at last I must have fainted, as I remembered nothing more till I found myself in bed, and awoke with my poor posteriors tremendously bruised and sore, and it was nearly a fortnight before I got rid of all the marks of that severe whipping.

After they reckoned me amongst the big girls, and I got a jolly bedfellow, whom I will call Alice Marchmont, a beautiful, fair girl, with a plump figure, large sensuous eyes, and flesh as firm and smooth as ivory. She seemed to take a great fancy to me, and the second night I slept with her (we had a small room to ourselves) she kissed and hugged me so lovingly that I felt slightly confused at first, as she took such liberties with me, my heart was all in a flutter, and although the light was out, I felt my face covered with burning blushes as her hot kisses on my lips, and the searching gropings of her hands in the most private parts of my person, made me all atremble.

"How you shake, dear Beatrice," she answered. "What are you afraid of? you may feel me all over too; it is so nice. Put your tongue in my mouth, it is a great inducement to love and I do want to love you so, dear. Where's your hand? here, put it there; can't you feel the hair just beginning to grow on my pussey? Yours will come soon. Rub your finger on my crack, just there," so she initiated me into the art of frigging in the most tender loving manner.

As you may guess, I was an apt pupil, although so young. Her touches fired my blood, and the way she sucked my tongue seemed most delicious. "Ah! Oh! Rub harder, harder -quicker," she gasped, as she stiffened her limbs out with a kind of spasmodic shudder, and I felt my finger all wet with something warm and creamy. She covered me with kisses for a moment, and then lay quite still.

"What is it, Alice? How funny you are, and you have wetted my finger, you nasty girl," I whispered, laughing. "Go on tickling me with your fingers, I begin rather to like it."

"So you will, dear, soon, and love me for teaching you such a nice game," she replied, renewing her frigging operations, which gave me great pleasure so that I hardly knew what I was doing, and a most luscious longing sensation came over me. I begged her to shove her fingers right up. "Oh! Oh! How nice! Further! Harder!" and almost fainted with delight as she at last brought down my first maiden spend.

Next night we repeated our lascivious amusements, and she produced a thing like a sausage, made of soft kid leather, and stuffed out as hard as possible, which she asked me to push into her, and work up and down, whilst she frigged me as before, making me lay on the top of her, with my tongue in her mouth. It was delightful. I can't express her raptures, my movements with the instrument seemed to drive her into ecstasies of pleasure, she almost screamed as she clasped my body to hers, exclaiming, "Ah! Oh! You dear boy; you kill me with pleasure!" as she spent with extraordinary profusion all over my busy hand.

As soon as we had recovered our serenity a little, I asked her what she meant by calling me her dear boy.

"Ah! Beatrice," she replied, "I'm so sleepy now, but tomorrow night, I will tell you my story, and explain how it is that my pussey is able to take in that thing, whilst yours cannot at present; it will enlighten you a little more into the Philosophy of Life, my dear; now give me a kiss, and let us go to sleep to-night."

29

Alice Marchmont's Story

You may imagine I was anxious for the next morning to arrive. We were no sooner in our little sanctum, than I exclaimed, "Now, Alice, make haste into bed, I'm all impatient to hear your tale."

"You shall have it dear and my fingers, too, if you will but let me undress comfortably. I can't jump into bed anyhow; I must make the inspection of my little private curls first. What do you think of them, Beatrice? Off with your chemise; I want to compare our pusseys," said she, throwing off everything, and surveying her beautiful naked figure in the large cheval glass. I was soon beside her, equally denuded of covering. "What a delightfully pouting little slit you have, Beatrice," she exclaimed, patting my Mons Veneris. "We shall make a beautiful contrast, mine is a light blonde, and yours will be brunette. See my little curly parsley bed is already half-an-inch long."

She indulged in no end of exciting tricks, till at last my patience was exhausted, so slipping on my chemise de nuit, I bounced into bed, saying I believed it was all fudge about her having a tale to tell and that I would not let her love me again, till she had satisfied my curiosity.

"What bad manners to doubt my word," she cried, following me into bed, taking me by surprise, uncovered my bottom, and inflicted a smart little slapping, as she laughingly continued, "There, let that be a lesson to you not to doubt a young lady's word in future. Now you shall have my tale, although it would really serve you right to make you wait till to-morrow."

After a short pause, having settled ourselves lovingly in bed, she

30

began:

Once upon a time there was a young lady, of the name of Alice, her parents were rich, and lived in a beautiful house, surrounded by lovely gardens and a fine park, she had a brother about two years older than herself, but her mama was so fond of her (being an only daughter), that she never would allow her little girl out of her sight, unless William, the butler, had charge of her in her rambles about the grounds and park,

William was a handsome, good-looking man about thirty, and had been in the family ever since he was a boy. Now Alice, who was very fond of William, often sat on his knee as he was seated under a tree, or on a garden seat, when he would read to her fairy tales from her books. Their intimacy was so great that when they were alone, she would call him "dear old Willie," and treat him quite as an equal. Alice was quite an inquisitive girl, and would often put Mr. William to the blush by her curious enquiries about natural history affairs, and how animals had little ones, why the cock was so savage to the poor hens, jumping on their backs, and biting their heads with his sharp beak, &c. "My dear," he would say, "I'm not a hen or a cow; how should I know? don't ask such silly questions"; but Miss Alice was not so easily put off, she would reply, "Ah! Willie, you do know, and won't tell me, I insist upon knowing, &c.," but her efforts to obtain knowledge were quite fruitless.

This went on for some time till the little girl was within three or four months of her birthday, when a circumstance she had never taken any notice of before aroused her curiosity. It was that Mr. William, under pretense of seeing to his duties, was in the habit of secluding himself in his pantry, or closet, from seven to eight o'clock in the morning for about an hour before breakfast. If Alice ventured to tap at the door it was fastened inside, and admittance refused; the keyhole was so closed it was useless to try and look through that way, but it occurred to my little girl that perhaps she might be able to get a peep into that place of mystery if she could only get into a passage which passed behind Mr. William's pantry, and into which she knew it used to open by a half-glass door, now never used, as the passage was closed by a locked door at each end. This passage was lighted from the outside by a small window about four feet from the ground, fastened on the inside simply by a hook, which Alice, who mounted on a high stool, soon found she could open if she broke one of the small diamond panes of glass, which she did, and then waiting till the next morning felt sure she would be able to find out what Willie was always so busy about, and also that she could get in and out of the window unobserved by anyone, as it was quite screened from view by a thick shrubbery seldom entered by anyone.

Up betimes next day she told her lady's-maid she was going to enjoy the fresh air in the garden before breakfast, and then hurried off to her place of observation, and scrambled through the window regardless of dirt and dust, took off her boots as soon as she alighted in the disused passage, and silently crept up to the glass door, but to her chagrin found the panes so dirty as to be impervious to sight; however, she was so far lucky as to find a fine large keyhole quite clear, and two or three cracks in the woodwork, so that she could see nearly every part of the place, which was full of light from a skylight overhead. Mr. William was not there, but soon made his appearance, bringing a great basket of plate, which had been used the previous day, and for a few minutes was really busy looking in his pantry book, and counting spoons, forks, &c., but was soon finished, and began to look at a little book, which he took from a drawer. Just then, Lucy, one of the prettiest housemaids, a dark beauty of about eighteen, entered the room without ceremony, saying, "Here's some of your plate off the sideboard. Where's your eyes, Mr. William, not to gather up all as you ought to do?" William's eyes seemed to beam with delight as he caught herround the waist, and gave her a luscious kiss on her cheek, saying: "Why, I keep them for you, dear, I knew you would bring the plate"; then showing the book, "What do you think of that position, dear? How would you like it so?"

Although pleased, the girl blushed up to the roots of her hair as she looked at the picture. The book dropped to the floor, and William pulled her on to his knee, and tried to put his hand up her clothes. "Ah! No! No!" she cried, in a low voice; "you know I can't to-day, but perhaps I can tomorrow; you must be good to-day, sir. Don't stick up your impudent head like that. There-there-there's a squeeze for you; now I must be off," she said, putting her hand down into his lap, where it could not be seen what she was after. In a second or two she jumped up, and in spite of his efforts to detain her, escaped from the pantry. William, evidently in a great state of excitement, subsided on to a sofa, muttering, "The little witch, what a devil she is; I can't help myself, but she will be all right to-morrow." Alice, who was intently observing everything, was shocked and surprised to see his trousers all unbuttoned in front, and a great long fleshy-looking thing sticking out, seemingly hard and stiff, with a ruby-coloured head. Mr, William took hold of it with one hand, apparently for the purpose of placing it in his breeches, but he seemed to hesitate, and closing his right hand upon the shaft, rubbed it up and down. "Ah! What a fool I am to let her excite me so. Oh! Oh! I can't help it; I must." He seemed to sigh as his hand increased its rapid motion. His face flushed, and his eyes seemed ready to start from his head, and in a few moments something spurted from his instrument, the drops falling over his hands and legs, some even a yard or two over the floor. This seemed to finish his ecstasy. He sank back quite listless for a few minutes, and then rousing himself, wiped his hands on a towel, cleared up every drop of the mess, and left the pantry. Alice was all over in a burning heat from what she had seen but instinctively felt that the mystery was only half unravelled, and promised herself to be there and see what William and Lucy would do next day. Mr. William took her for a walk as usual, and read to her, whilst she sat on his knee, and Alice wondered what could have become of that great stiff thing which she had seen in the morning. With the utmost apparent innocence, her hands touched him casually, where she hoped to feel the monster, but only resulted in feeling a rather soft kind of bunch in his pocket.

Another morning arrived to find Alice at her post behind the disused glass door, and she soon saw Mr. William bring in his plate, but he put it aside, and seemed all impatient for Lucy's arrival. "Ah!" he murmurs. "I'm as stiff as a rolling pin at the very thought of the saucy darling," but his ideas were cut short by the appearance of Lucy herself, who care-fully bolted the door inside. Then rushing into his arms, she covered him with kisses, exclaiming, in a low voice, "Ah! How I have longed for him these three or four days. What a shame women should be stopped in that way from enjoying themselves once a month. How is he this morning?" as her hands nervously unbuttoned Mr. William's trousers, and grasped his ready truncheon.

"What a hurry you are in, Lucy!" gasped her lover, as she almost stifled him with her kisses. "Don't spoil it all by your impatience; I must have my kiss first."

With a gentle effort he reclined her backwards on a sofa, and raised her clothes till Alice had a full view of a splendid pair of plump, white legs; but what rivetted her gaze most was the luscious looking, pouting lips of Lucy's cunny, quite vermilion in colour, and slightly gaping open, in a most inviting manner, as her legs were wide apart; her Mons Veneris being covered with a profusion of beautiful curly black hair.

The butler was down on his knees in a moment, and glued his lips to her crack, sucking and kissing furiously, to the infinite delight of the girl, who sighed and wriggled with pleasure; till at last Mr. William could no longer restrain himself, but getting up upon his knees between Lucy's legs, he brought his shaft to the charge, and to Alice's astonishment, fairly ran it right into the gaping crack, till it was all lost in her belly; they laid still for a few moments, enjoying the conjunction of their persons till Lucy heaved up her bottom, and the butler responded to it by a shove, then they commenced a most exciting struggle. Alice could see the manly shaft as it worked in and out of her sheath, glistening with lubricity, whilst the lips of her cunny seemed to cling to it each time of withdrawal, as if afraid of losing such a delightful sugar stick; but this did not last long, their movements got more and more furious, till at last both seemed to meet in a spasmodic embrace, as they almost fainted in each other's arms, and Alice could see a profusion of creamy moisture oozing from the crack of Lucy, as they both lay in a kind of lethargy of enjoyment after their battle of love.

Mr. William was the first to break the silence: "Lucy, will you look in to-morrow, dear; you know that old spy, Mary, will be back from her holiday in a day or two, and then we shan't often have a chance."

Lucy,-"Ah; you rogue, I mean to have a little more now, I don't care if we're caught; I must have it," she said, squeezing him with her arms and gluing her lips to his, as she threw her beautiful legs right over his buttocks, and commenced the engagement once more by rapidly heaving her bottom; in fact, although he was a fine man, the weight of his body seemed as nothing in her amorous excitement.

The butler's excuses and pleading of fear, in case he was missed,

&c., were all of no avail; she fairly drove him on, and he was soon as furiously excited as herself, and with a profusion of sighs, expressions of pleasure, endearment, &c., they soon died away again into a state of short voluptuous oblivion. However, Mr. William was too nervous and afraid to let her lay long; he withdrew his instrument from her foaming cunny, just as it was all slimy and glistening with the mingled juices of their love; but what a contrast to its former state, as Alice now beheld it much reduced in size, and already drooping its fiery head.

Lucy jumped up and let down her clothes, but kneeling on the floor before her lover, she took hold of his limp affair, and gave it a most luscious sucking, to the great delight of Mr. William, whose face flushed again with pleasure, and as soon as Lucy had done with her sucking kiss, Alice saw that his instrument was again stiff and ready for a renewal of their joys.

Lucy, laughing in a low tone.-"There, my boy, I'll leave you like that; think of me till to-morrow; I couldn't help giving the darling a good suck after the exquisite pleasure he had afforded me, it's like being in heaven for a little while."

With a last kiss on the lips as they parted, and Mr. William again locked his door, whilst Alice made good her retreat to prepare herself for breakfast.

It was a fine warm morning in May, and soon after breakfast Alice, with William for her guardian, set off for a ramble in the park, her blood was in a boil, and she longed to experience the joys she was sure Lucy had been surfeited with; they sauntered down to the lake, and she asked William to give her a row in the boat; he unlocked the boat-house, and handed her into a nice, broad, comfortable skiff, well furnished with soft seats and cushions.

"How nice to be here, in the shade," said Alice; "come into the boat, Willie, we will sit in it a little while, and you shall read to me before we have a row."

"Just as you please, Miss Alice," he replied, with unwonted deference, stepping into the boat, and sitting down in the stern sheets.

"Ah my head aches a little, let me recline it in your lap," said Alice, throwing off her hat, and stretching herself along on a cushion. "Why are you so precise this morning, Willie? You know I don't like to be called Miss, you can keep that for Lucy." Then noticing his confusion, "You may blush, sir, I could make you sink into your shoes if you only knew all I have seen between you and Miss Lucy."

Alice reclined her head in a languid manner on his lap, looking up and enjoying the confusion she had thrown him into; then designedly resting one hand on the lump which he seemed to have in his pocket, as if to support herself a little, she continued: "Do you think, Willie, I shall ever have as fine legs as Lucy? Don't you think I ought soon to have long dresses, sir! I'm getting quite bashful about showing my calves so much," The butler had hard work to recover his composure, the vivid recollection of the luscious episode with Lucy before breakfast was so fresh in his mind that Alice's allusions to her, and the soft girlish hand resting on his privates (even although he thought her as innocent as a lamb) raised an utter of desire in his feverish blood, which he tried to allay as much as possible, but little by little the unruly member began to swell, till he was sure she must feel it throb under her hand. With an effort he slightly shifted himself, so as to remove her hand lower down on to the thigh, as he answered as gravely as possible (feeling assured Alice could know nothing): "You're making game of me this morning. Don't you wish me to read, Alice?"

Alice, excitedly, with an unusual flush on her face.-"You naughty man, you shall tell me what I want to know this time. How do babies come? What is the parsley bed, the nurses and doctors say they come out of? Is it not a curly lot of hair at the bottom of the woman's belly? I know that's what Lucy's got, and I've seen you kiss it, sir!"

(To be continued)

A PROLOGUE

*

*Spoke by Miss Bella de Lancy, on her retiring from the Stage to open
a Fashionable Bawdy House*

(Written by S. Johnson, LL.D.)

When cunt first triumphed (as the learned suppose)
O'er failing pricks, Immortal Dildo rose,
From fucks unnumbered, still erect he drew,
Exhausted cunts, and then demanded new;
Dame Nature saw him spurn her bounded reign,
And panting pricks toiled after him in vain;
The laxest folds, the deepest depths he filled;
The juiciest drained; the toughest hymens drilled.
The fair lay gasping with distended limbs,
And unremitting cockstands stormed their quims.
Then Frigging came, instructed from the school,
And scorned the aid of India-rubber tool .
With restless finger, fired the dormant blood,
Till Clitoris rose, sly, peeping thro' her hood.
Gently was worked this titillating art,
It broke no hymen, and scarce stretched the part;
Yet lured its votaries to a sudden doom,
And stamped Consumption's flush on Beauty's bloom.
Sweet Gamahuche found softer ways to fame,
It asked not Dildo's art, nor Frigging's flame.

Tongue, not prick, now probes the central hole,
And mouth, not cunt, becomes prick's destined goal.
It always found a sympathetic friend;
And pleased limp pricks, and those who could not spend,
No tedious wait, for laboured stand, delays
The hot and pouting cunt, which tongue allays.
The taste was luscious, tho' the smell was strong;
The fuck was easy, and would last so long;
Til wearied tongues found gamahuching cloy,
And pricks, and cunts, grew callous to the joy.
Then dulled by frigging, by mock pricks enlarged,
Her noble duties Cunt but ill discharged.
Her nymphæ drooped, her devil's bite grew weak,
And twice two pricks might flounder in her creek;
Till all the edge was taken off the bliss,
And Cunt's sole occupation was to piss.
Forced from her former joys, with scoft and brunt,
She saw great Arsehole lay the ghost Cunt
Exulting buggers hailed the joyful day,
And piles and homerrids confirmed his sway.
But who lust's future fancies can explore,
And mark the whimsies that remain in store?
Perhaps it shall be deemed a lover's treat,
To suck the flowering quims of mares in heat;
Perhaps, where beauty held unequalled sway,
A Cochin fowl shall rival Mabel Grey;
Nobles be rained by the Hyaena's smile,
And Seals get short engagements from th' Argyle.
Hard is her lot, that here by Fortune placed,
Must watch the wild vicissitudes of taste;
Catch every whim, learn every bawdy trick,
And chase the new born bubbles of the prick;
Ah, let not Censure term our fate, our choice,
The Bawd but echoes back the public voice;
The Brothers laws, the Brothel's patrons give,
And those that live to please, must please to live;
Then purge these growing follies from your hearts,
And turn to female arms, and female arts;

'Tis yours this night, to bid the reign begin,
Of all the good old-fashioned ways to sin;
Clean, wholesome girls, with lip, tongue, cunt, and hand,
Shall raise, keep up, put in, take down a stand;
Your bottoms shall by lily hands be bled,
And birches blossom under every bed.

THE ORIGIN SPECIES

*

Air.-"Derry Down"

When Adam and Eve were first put into Eden,
They never once thought of that pleasant thing-breeding
Though they had not a rag to cover their front,
Adam sported his prick, and Eve sported her cunt.

Derry down.

Adam's prick was so thick and so long-such a teaser;
Eve's cunt was so hairy and fat-such a breezer;
Adam's thing was just formed any maiden to please,
And his bollocks hung down very near to his knees.

Derry down.

Eve played with his balls, and thought it no harm:
He fingered her quim and ne'er felt alarm;
He tickled her bubbies, she rubbed up his yard,
And yet for a fuck, why they felt no regard.

Derry down.

But when Mrs. Eve did taste of the fruit,
It was then that her eyes first beheld Adam's root;
Then he ate an apple, and after he had done't,

Why then he first found out the value of cunt.

Derry down.

Then they say they made fig leaves, that's fiddle-de-dee.
He wanted a quim, and quite ready was she;
They gazed on their privates with mutual delight,
And she soon found a hole to put jock out of sight!

Derry down.

Then Adam soon laid Mrs. Eve on the grass,
He pop't in his prick, she heaved up her arse;
He wriggled, she wiggled, they both stuck to one tether
And she tickled his balls, till they both came together!

Derry down.

Since then, all her children are filled with desire,
And the women a stiff-standing prick all require!
And no son of Adam will e'er take affront,
For where is the man that can live without cunt.

Derry down.

THE WANTON LASS

*

Air.-"Derry Down"

There was a lass they called bonny Bet,
With a jolly fat arse, and a cunt black as jet;
Her quim had long itched, and she wanted, I vow,
A jolly good fucking, but couldn't tell how.

Derry down.

She thought of a plan that might serve as the same,
That herself she might shag without any shame;
So a carrot she got, with a point rather blunt,
And she ramm'd it and jamm'd it three parts up her cunt.

Derry down.

She liked it so well that she oft used to do it,
Till at length the poor girl had occasion to rue it;
For one day, when amusing herself with this whim,
The carrot it snapped, and part stuck in her quim.

Derry down.

She went almost mad with vexation at this,
Indeed it was time, the poor girl couldn't piss.
The lass was in torture, no rest had poor Bet,

42

So at last an old doctor she was forced to get.

Derry down.

The doctor he came, and she told him the case,
Then with spectacles on, and a very long face,
He bid her turn up, though she scarcely was able,
And pull up her petticoats over her navel.

Derry down.

Her clouts she held up, round her belly so plump,
And he gave her fat arse such a hell of a thump,
That he made her cry out, tho' he did it so neat,
And away flew the carrot bang into the street.

Derry down.

Now a sweep passing by, he saw it come down,
Picked it up and he ate it, and said with a frown,
By God! it's not right, it's a damned shame, I say,
That people should throw buttered carrots away.

Derry down.

THE MEETING OF THE WATERS

*

A Parody on Moore's Melody

There is not in this wide world a valley so sweet,
As that vale where the thighs of a pretty girl meet:
Oh, the last ray of feeling and life must depart,
Ere the bloom of that valley shall fade from my heart.
Yet it is not that Nature has shed o'er the scene,
The purest of red, the most delicate skin,
'Tis not the sweet smell of the genial hill;
Ah, no! it is something more exquisite still.
'Tis because the last favours of woman are there,
Which make every part of her body more dear.
We feel how the charms of Nature improve,
When we bathe in the spendings of her whom we love.

LOVE

Nature, everywhere the same,
Imparts to man a lustful flame;
In Russian snow or Indian fire,
All men alike indulge desire,
All alike, feel passion's heat,
All alike, enjoyment greet,
So that wheresoe'er you go,
Still the same voluptuous glow
Throbs through every purple vein,
Thirsts enjoyment to obtain;
'Mongst the dark, or with the fair,
Woman is empress everywhere.

THE PLEASURES OF LOVE

Pressed in the arms of him I so adored,
The keeper of my charms, my pride, my lord!
By day experiencing each sweet delight,
And meeting endless transports every night
When on our downy bed we fondly lay,
Heating each other by our am'rous play;
Till Nature, yielding to the luscious game,
Would fierce desire and quenchless lust inflame!
Oh! then we join'd in love's most warm embrace,
And pressed soft kisses on our every grace!
Around my form his pliant limbs entwined,
Love's seat of bliss to him I then resigned!
We pant, we throb, we both convulsive start!
Heavens! then what passions thro' our fibres dart!
We heave, we wriggle, bite, laugh, tremble, sigh!
We taste Elysian bliss-we fondle-die.

THE RIVAL TOASTS

An English and an American vessel of war being in port together, Captain Balls, of the former, invited the officers of the Yankee frigate to dine in board of his ship, but stipulated, in order to avoid any unpleasantness, that no offensive or personal toasts should be proposed, to which the Americans cheerfully assented. However, after dinner, during dessert, when the conversation happened to turn warmly upon the respective merits of the two nations, a Yankee officer suddenly stood up, and said he wished to propose a toast, which he should take as a personal offense if anyone refused to drink it.

Captain B. mildly expressed a hope that it was nothing offensive, but consented to drink to whatever it might be, with the proviso that, if he thought fit to do so, he should propose another afterwards.

Then shouted the American, exultingly: "Here's to the glorious American flag: Stars to enlighten all nations, and Stripes to flog them."

Captain B. drained a bumper to the American's toast; then turning to the old ship's steward, standing behind his chair, said quietly: "You can beat that, can't you, Jack?"

"Ay! Aye! Sir! If you fill me a stiff'un."

The Captain mixed him a good swig of hot and strong. Then handing the steward the glass, he thundered out: "Silence for Jack's toast, and any gentleman here present, refusing to drink to it, I shall not take it as a personal offense, but at once order the gunner's mate to give him three dozen. Now then, Jack."

Jack, with a grim smile, and bowing to the Yankee officer, said: "Then here's to the ramping, roaring British Lion, who shits on the stars, and wipes his arse on the stripes."

NURSERY RHYMES

There was a young man of Bombay,
Who fashioned a cunt out of clay;
But the heat of his prick
Turned it into a brick,
And chafed all his foreskin away.
There was a young man of Peru,
Who had nothing whatever to do;
So he took out his carrot
And buggered his parrot,
And sent the result to the Zoo.
There was a young girl of Ostend,
Who her maidenhead tried to defend,
But a Chasseur d'Afrique inserted his prick,
And taught that ex-maid how to spend.
There was a young man of Calcutta,
Who tried to write "Cunt" on a shutter.
When he got to C-U,
A pious Hindoo
Knocked him arse over head in the gutter.
There was a young man of Ostend,
Whose wife caught him fucking her friend;
"It's no use, my duck,
Interrupting our fuck,
For I'm damned if I draw till I spend."
There was a young man of Wood Green,

Who tried to fart "God Save the Queen."
When he reached the soprano,
He shot his guano,
And his breeches weren't fit to be seen.
There was a young man of Dundee,
Who one night went out on the spree;
He wound up his clock
With the tip of his cock,
And buggered himself with the key.
There was a young lady of Troy,
Who invented a new kind of joy:
She sugared her thing
Both outside and in,
And then had it sucked by a boy.
There was a young man of Santander,
Who tried hard to bugger a gander;
But the virtuous bird
Plugged his arse with a turd,
And refused to such low tastes to pander.
There was a young lady of Hitchin,
Who was skrotching her cunt in the kitchen;
Her father said "Rose,
It's the crabs, I suppose."
"You're right, pa, the buggers are itching."
There was an old person of Sark,
Who buggered a pig in the dark;
The swine, in surprise,
Murmured "God blast your eyes,
Do you take me for Boulton or Park?"

AMEN

Oh! cunt is a kingdom, and prick is its lord;
A whore is a slave, and her mistress a bawd;
Her quim is her freehold, which brings in her rent;
Where you pay when you enter, and leave when you've spent.

VOLUME II

* * * * *

Published Monthly

Aug. 1879

SUB-UMBRA, OR SPORT AMONG THE SHE-NOODLES

(continued)

Annie was ready to faint as she screamed, "Walter! Walter! Save me from the horrid beast!" I comforted and reassured her as well as I was able, and seeing that we were on the safe side of the gate, a few loving kisses soon set her all right. We continued our walk, and soon spying out a favourable shady spot, I said: "Come, Annie dear, let us sit down and recover from the startling interruption; I am sure, dear, you must still feel very agitated, besides I must get you now to compensate me for (he rude disappointment."

She seemed to know that her hour had come; the hot blushes swept in crimson waves across her lovely face, as she cast down her eyes, and permitted me to draw her down by my side on a mossy knoll, and we lay side by side, my lips glued to hers in a most ardent embrace.

"Annie! Oh! Annie!" I gasped, "Give me the tip of your tongue, love." She tipped me the velvet without the slightest hesitation, drawing, at the same time, what seemed a deep sigh of delightful anticipation as she yielded to my slightest wish. I had one arm under her head, and with the other I gently removed her hat, and threw aside my own golgotha, kissing and sucking at her delicious tongue all the while. Then I placed one of her hands on my ready cock, which was in a bursting state, saying, as I released her tongue for a moment: "There, Annie, take the dart of love in your hand." She grasped it nervously, as she softly murmured: "Oh, Walter, I'm so afraid; and yet-oh yet, dearest, I feel, I die, I must taste the sweets of love, this forbidden fruit," her voice sinking almost to a whisper, as she pressed and passed her hand up and down my shaft. My hand was also busy finding its way under her clothes as I again glued my mouth to hers, and sucked at her tongue till I could feel her vibrate all over with the excess of her emotion. My hand, which had taken possession of the seat of bliss, being fairly deluged with her warm glutinous spendings.

"My love; my life! I must kiss you there, and taste the nectar of love." I exclaimed, as I snatched my lips from hers, and reversing my position, buried my face between her un-resisting thighs. I licked up the luscious spendings with rapturous delight from the lips of her tight lime cunny, then my tongue found its way further, till it tickled her sensitive clitoris, and put her into a frenzy of mad desire for still further enjoyment; she twisted her legs over my head, squeezing my head between her firm plump thighs in an ecstasy of delight.

Wetting my finger in her luscious crack, I easily inserted it in her beautifully wrinkled brown bum-hole, and keeping my tongue busy in titillating the stiff little clitoris, I worked her up into such a furious state of desire that she clutched my cock and brought it to her mouth, as I lay over her to give her the chance of doing so; she rolled her tongue round the purple head, and I could also feel the loving playful bite of her pearly teeth. It was the acme of erotic enjoyment. She came again in another luscious flood of spendings, whilst she eagerly sucked every drop of my sperm as it burst from my excited prick.

We both nearly fainted from the excess of our emotions, and lay quite exhausted for a few moments, till I felt her dear lips again pressing and sucking my engine of love. The effect was electric; I was as stiff as ever.

"Now, darling, for the real stroke of love." I exclaimed. Shifting my position, and parting her quivering thighs, so that I could kneel between them. My knees were placed upon her skirts so as to preserve them from the grass stain. She lay before me in a delightful state of anticipation, her beautiful face all blushes of shame, and the closed eyelids, fringed with their long dark lashes, her lips slightly open, and the finely developed, firm, plump globes of her bosom heaving in a state of tumultuous excitement. It was ravishing, I felt mad with lust, and could no longer put off the actual consummation. I could not contain myself. Alas; poor maidenhead! Alas! for your virginity! I brought my cock to the charge, presented the head just slightly between the lips of her vagina. A shudder of delight seemed to pass through her frame at the touch of my weapon, as her eyes opened, and she whispered, with a soft, loving smile, "I know it will hurt, but Walter, dear Walter, be both firm and kind. I must have it, if it kills me," Throwing her arms around my neck, she drew my lips to hers, as she thrust her tongue into my mouth with all the abandon of love, and shoved up her bottom to meet my charge.

I placed one hand under her buttocks, whilst, with the other, I kept my affair straight to the mark; then pushing vigorously, the head entered about an inch, till it was chock up to the opposing hymen. She gave a start of pain, but her eyes gazed into mine with a most encouraging look.

"Throw your legs over my back, dear," I gasped, scarcely relinquishing her tongue for a moment. Her lovely thighs turned round me in a spasmodic frenzy of determination to bear the worst. I gave a ruthless push, just as her bottom heaved up to meet me, and the deed was done. King Priapus had burst through all obstacles to our enjoyment. She gave a subdued shriek of agonized pain, and I felt myself throbbing in possession of her inmost charms.

"You darling! You love me! My brave Annie, how well you stood the pain. Let us lay still for a moment or two, and then for the joys of love." I exclaimed, as I kissed her face, forehead, eyes, and mouth in a transport of delight, at feeling the victory so soon accomplished.

Presently I could feel the tight sheath of her vagina contracting on my cock in the most delicious manner. This challenge was too much for my impetuous steed. He gave a gentle thrust. I could see by the spasm of pain which passed over her beautiful face, that it was still painful to her, but, restraining my ardour, I worked very gently, although my lust was so maddening that I could not restrain a copious spend; so I sank on her bosom in love's delicious lethargy.

It was only for a few moments, I could feel her tremble beneath me with voluptuous ardour, and the sheath being now well lubricated, we commenced a delightful bout of ecstatic fucking. All her pain was forgotten, the wounded parts soothed by the flow of my semen now only revelled in the delightful friction of love; she seemed to boil over in spendings, my delighted cock revelled in it, as he thrust in and out with all my manly vigour; we spent three or four times in a delirium of voluptuousness, till I was fairly vanquished by her impetuosity, and begged her to be moderate, and not to injure herself by excessive enjoyment

"Oh! can it be possible to hurt one's self by such a delightful pleasure?" she sighed, then seeing me withdraw my limp tool from her still longing cunt, she smiled archly, as she said with a blush, "Pardon my rudeness, dear Walter, but I fear it is you who are most injured after all; look at your bloodstained affair."

"You lovely little simpleton," I said, kissing her rapturously, "that's your own virgin blood; let me wipe you, darling," as I gently applied my handkerchief to her pouting slit, and afterwards to my own cock. "This, dearest Annie, I shall treasure up as the proofs of your virgin love, so delightfully surrendered to me this day," exhibiting the ensanguined mouchoir to her gaze.

We now arose from our soft mossy bed, and mutually assisted each other to remove all traces of our love engagement. Then we walked on, and I enlightened the dear girl into all the arts and practices of love. "Do you think," I remarked, "that your sisters or Frank have any idea of what the joys of love are like?"

"I believe they would enter into it as ardently as I do, if they were but once initiated," she replied. "I have often heard Frank say when kissing us, that we made him burn all over"; and then blushing deeply as her eyes met mine, "Oh! dear Walter, I'm afraid you will think we are awfully rude girls, but when we go to bed at night, myself and sisters often compare our budding charms, and crack little jokes about the growing curls of mine and Sophie's slits, and the hairless little pussey of Polly; we have such games of slapping, and romps too, sometimes; it has often made me feel a kind of all-overishness of feverish excitement I could not understand, but thanks to you, love, I can make it all out now; I wish you could only get a peep at us, dear,"

"Perhaps it might be managed; you know my room is next to yours, I could hear you laughing and having a game last night." "I know we did, we had such fun," she replied, "it was Polly trying to put my pussey in curl papers, but how can you manage it, dear?"

Seeing she fully entered into my plans for enjoyment, we consulted together, and at last I hit upon an idea which I thought might work very well; it was that I should first sound Frank and enlighten him a little into the ways of love, and then as soon as he was ripe for our purpose, we would surprise the three sisters whilst naked bathing, and slap their naked bottoms all round; that Annie should encourage her sisters to help her in tearing off all our clothes, and then we could indulge in a general romp of love.

Annie was delighted at the idea, and I promised the very next day to begin with Frank, or perhaps that very afternoon if I got a chance.

We returned to the house, Annie's cheeks blushing and carrying a beautiful flush of health, and her mama remarked that our walk had evidently done her very great good, little guessing that her daughter, like our first mother Eve, had that morning tasted of the forbidden fruit, and was greatly enlightened and enlivened thereby.

After luncheon I asked Frank to smoke a cigarette in my room, which he at once complied with.

As soon as I had closed the door, I said, "Old fellow, did you ever see Fanny Hill, a beautiful book of love and pleasure?"

"What, a smutty book, I suppose you mean? No, Walter, but if you have got it I should wonderfully like to look at it," he said, his eyes sparkling with animation.

"Here it is, my boy, only I hope it won't excite you too much; you can look it over by yourself, as I read the Times," said I, taking it out of my dressing-case, and handing it to his eager grasp.

He sat close to me in an easy lounging chair, and I watched him narrowly as he turned over the pages and gloated over the beautiful plates; his prick hardened in his breeches till it was quite stiff and rampant.

"Ha! Ha!! Ha!!! old fellow, I thought it would fetch you out!" I said, laying my hand upon his cock. "By Jove, Frank! what a tosser yours has grown since we used to play in bed together a long time ago. I'll lock the door, we must compare our parts, I think mine is nearly as big as yours."

He made no remark, but I could see he was greatly excited by the book. Having locked the door, I leant over his shoulder and made my remarks upon the plates as he turned them over. At length (he book dropped from his hands, and his excited gaze was rivetted on my bursting breeches.

"Why, Walter, you are as bad as I am," he said, with a laugh, "let's see which is the biggest," pulling out his hard, stiff prick, and then laying his hands on me pulled my affair out to look at.

We handled each other in an ecstasy of delight, which ended in our throwing off all our clothes, and having a mutual fuck between our thighs on the bed; we spent in rapture, and after a long dalliance he entered into my plans, and we determined to have a lark with the girls as soon as we could get a chance. Of course I was mum as to what had passed between Annie and myself.

(To be continued.)

MISS COOTE'S CONFESSION, OR THE VOLUPTUOUS EXPERIENCES OF AN OLD MAID

In a series of Letters to Lady Friend.

*

Letter II

My Dear Nellie,

To continue my tale where I left off. Jane and I had some further conversation next morning, which, to the best of my recollection, was as follows:-

ROSA.-"So, Jane, you have been whipped, have you. What was it for?"

JANE.-"The first time was for being seen walking with a young man coming from church. The General said I had never been, and only pretended to be religious for the chance of gadding about with young fellows, which must be checked, or I should be ruined."

ROSA.-"Well; didn't you feel revengeful at being whipped for that?"

JANE.-"So I did, but forgot all about it in the delight I had in seeing Jemima well cut up. Oh, she did just catch it, I can tell you; but she's as strong and hard as leather."

ROSA.-"So I could forget and forgive too, if I could but cut you all up well. I've got a good mind to begin with you, Jane, when I don't feel quite so sore."

JANE.-"Ah! But I know you hate Jemima, and would rather see

her triced up to the horse. Perhaps we shall be able to get her into a scrape between us, if we put our heads together."

ROSA.-"Oh! I you sly girl. Don't you think I'll let you off, much as I long to repay the others. Just wait till I feel well enough, and I'll settle you first. There will be plenty of opportunities, as you are to sleep with me in my room every night. I haven't forgotten how you persuaded me to dress for dinner, when you knew, all the time, what was coming."

JANE.-"Dear Miss Rosie, I couldn't help it. Mrs. Mansell sent me up to dress you. The old General put it off till after dinner, as he likes to see the culprits dressed as nicely as possible. If he punished any of us, we have to attend punishment drill in our very best clothes, and if they get damaged, Mrs. Mansell soon fits us out again, so we don't lose much by a good birching. I have known Jemima to get into trouble so as to damage her things, but Sir Eyre made her smart well for them."

I was very sore for several days, but managed to make and secrete a fine bunch of twigs, ready for Miss Jane when she would little expect it. In fact, she did not know I had been into the garden or out of the house. Of course she was a much stronger and bigger girl than myself, so I should have to secure her by some stratagem. I let her think I had quite forgotten my threat, but one evening, just as we were both undressed for bed, I said, "Jane, did Mrs. Mansell or Jemima ever birch you without grandfather knowing it?"

JANE.-"Yes, dear Miss Rosie, they've served me out shamefully, more than once."

ROSA.-"How did they manage that?"

JANE.-"Why, I was tied by my hands to the foot of the bedstead."

ROSA.-"Oh! Do show me, and let me tie you up to see how it all looked."

JANE.-"Very well; if it's any pleasure to you, Miss."

ROSA.-"What shall I tie you up with? You're as strong as Samson."

JANE.-"A couple of handkerchiefs will do, and there's a small comforter to tie my legs."

By her directions I soon had her hands tied to the two knobs at the foot of the bed, and her feet stretched out a little behind were secured to the legs of. the table.

59

"Oh! My!" said Jane. "You have fixed me tight. What did you tie so hard for? I can't get away till you release me."

"Stay! Stay!" I cried. "I must see you quite prepared now you are properly fixed up"; and I quickly turned up her nightdress and secured it well above her waist, so as to expose her plump bottom and delicately mossed front to my astonished gaze.

"Oh! What a beauty you are, Jane," said I, kissing her, "and you know I love you, but your naughty little bum-be-dee must be punished. It is a painful duty, but I'll let you see it's no joke, Miss. Look, what a fine swishtail I've got," producing my rod.

"Mercy! Mercy!" cried Jane. "Dear Miss Rosie, you won't beat me; I've always been so kind to you!"

"It won't do, Jane, I must do my duty. You were one of the lot against me, and the first I can catch. It may be years before I can pay off the others."

The sight of her beautiful posteriors filled me with a gloating desire to exercise my skill upon them, and see a little of what I had to feel myself. Nervously grasping my birch, without further delay, I commenced the assault by some sharp strokes, each blow deepening the rosy tints to a deeper red.

"Ah! Ah! What a shame. You're as bad as the old General, you little witch, to take me so by surprise."

"You don't seem at all sorry, Miss," I cried; "but I'll try and bring down your impudence; in fact, I begin to think you are one of the worst of them, and only acted the hypocrite, with your pretended compassion, when you were, in reality, it all the time. But it's my turn now. Of course, you were too strong for me, unless I had trapped you so nicely. How do you like it, Miss Jane?" All this time I kept on, whisk, whisk, whisk, in quick succession, till her bottom began to look quite interesting.

"You little wretch! You vixen!" gasped Jane. "Your grandfather shall hear of this."

"That's your game, is it, Miss Tell-tale. At any rate, you'll be well paid first;" I replied. The sight of her buttocks only seemed to add to my energy, and it was quite a thrill of pleasure when I first saw the blood come. She writhed and wriggled with suppressed sighs and ahs, but each time she gave utterance to any expression, it seemed only for the purpose of irritating me more and more. My excitement became intense, the cruel havoc seemed to be an immense satisfaction to me, and her bottom really was in deplorable state through my inconsiderate fury. At last, quite worn put and fatigued, I could hold the rod no longer, and my passion melted into love and pity, as I saw her in an apparently listless and fainting condition, with drooping head, eyes closed, and hands clenched.

The worn-out birch was dropped, and kissing her tenderly, I sobbed out, "Jane, dear, Jane, I both love and forgive you now, and you will find me as tender to you as you were to me after my flogging."

Her hands and feet were soon released, when to my astonishment, she threw her arms round my neck as with sparkling eyes and a luscious kiss she said softly, "And I forgive you too, Miss Rosie, for you don't know what pleasure you have given me, the last few moments have been bliss indeed."

This was all a puzzle to me at the time, but I understood it well enough afterwards. She made quite light of her bruised bottom, saying, "What was awful to you was nothing to me, Miss Rosie, I am so much older and tougher; besides, the first time is always the worst; it was too bad of Sir Eyre to cut you up as he did, but your obstinacy made him forget himself; you'll grow to like it as I do."

This and much more in the same strain passed as we bathed and soothed the irritated parts, and we finally fell asleep with a promise from me to let her give me a pleasant lesson in a day or two.

Things went on smoothly for a few days, my punishment had been too severe for me to lightly dare a second engagement with the General; still I burned for a chance to avenge myself on anyone but Jane, who was now my bosom friend. We discussed all sorts of schemes for getting anyone but ourselves into trouble, but to no purpose. The old gentleman often cautioned me to take care, as the next time he should not fail to make me cry, "Peccavi."

One fine afternoon, however, being in the garden with the housekeeper, I remarked to her, "What a pity it was grand-father let the nectarines hang and spoil, and no one allowed to taste them."

"My dear," said Mrs. Mansell, "if you take two or three he'll never miss them, only you must not tell that I said so, it's a shame to let them rot."

"But, Mrs. Mansell, that would be stealing," I replied.

"When nothing's lost nothing can have been stolen; it's only a false sense of honesty, and you, the little mistress of the house," she urged.

"Well, you are the serpent, and I'm Eve, I suppose; they really do look delicious, and you won't tell, will you?" I asked in my simplicity; so the fruit was plucked, and Mrs. Mansell helped to eat it, which put me quite at my ease.

Just before dinner next day we were surprised by the General calling us all into his sitting-room, "How's this, Mrs. Mansell?" he said, looking fearfully angry. "I can't leave my keys in the lock of that cabinet without someone tasting my ram; I've long known there was a sly sipping thief about, so I have been sly too. Finding it was the rum that was most approved, the last time the decanter was filled I put a little scratch with my diamond ring, to mark the height of the liquor in the bottle, and have only used the brandy for myself. Look! whoever it is has got through nearly a pint in three or four days. Come here, Rosa, now Mrs. Mansell, and now Jemima," said he, sternly, smelling the breath of each in turn.

"Woman," he said, as she faltered and hesitated to undergo this ordeal, "I don't think you were a sneaking thief, if you really wanted a little spirit, Mrs. Mansell would have let you have it, I dare say, as you have been with us some years, and we don't like change, but you shall be cured of thieving tomorrow; you should have been well thrashed at once, but we have a friend to dinner this evening, it will do you good to wait and think of what's coming. Be off, now, and mind the dinner's served up properly or you'll catch it in Indian style tomorrow, and be a curried chicken if ever you were."

Our visitor was an old fox-hunting colonel, our nearest neighbour, and my spirits were so elated at the prospect of Jemima's punishment that it seemed to me the pleasantest evening I had ever spent in that house.

All next day grandfather spent looking over the garden, and a presentiment came over me that the nectarines would be missed; if he had been so cunning in one thing, he might be in another.

My fears were only too well founded, for catching sight of me with the housekeeper, cutting a nosegay for the criminal's wear, he said, "Mrs. Mansell, you had better make another bouquet whilst you are about it, someone has been at the nectarines; do you know anything about it, Rosa?"

"Oh! Grandfather, you know I was strictly forbidden to touch the fruit," said I, as innocently as possible.

"Mrs. Mansell, do you know anything of it, as she won't, give a direct answer," said he, eyeing me sternly.

I was covered with confusion, and to make it worse, Mrs. Mansell with affected reluctance to tell an untruth, confessed the whole affair.

"Upon my word, a nice honest lot you all are, as I dare say Jane is like the rest; Mrs. Mansell, I'm astonished at you, and I think your punishment will be enough, when you consider how seriously I look upon such things, but as to that girl Rosa, prevarication is worse than a lie, such cunning in one so young is frightful, but we'll settle Jemima first, and then think of what's to be done."

Left in this state of uncertainty, I fled to Jane for consolation, who assured me it was a good thing Jemima stood first, as the old man would get exhausted, and perhaps let me off lightly, if I screamed and begged for mercy.

Thus encouraged, I managed to eat a good dinner, and took an extra glass of wine on the sly (I was only supposed to take one). Thus fortified I marched to the punishment drill with great confidence, especially as I so wished to see Jemima well thrashed.

When first I set eyes upon her, as she curtseyed to the General, who was seated in the chair, rod in hand, her appearance struck me with admiration; rather above medium height, dark auburn hair, fresh colour, and sparkling blue eyes, low cut dark blue silk dress, almost revealing the splendours of her full rounded bosom, the large nosegay fixed rather on one side under her dimpled chin, pink satin high-heeled shoes, with silver buckles; she had short sleeves, but fawn-coloured gloves of kid, and a delicate net, covering her arms to the elbows, took off all coarseness of her red skin or hands.

"Prepare her at once," said the General, "she knows too well all I would say. Here, Rosie, hand me down that big bunch of birch, this little one is no use for her fat rump. Ha! ha! this is better," said he, whisking it about.

Jane and the housekeeper had already stripped off the blue silk, and were proceeding to remove the underskirts of white linen, trimmed with broad lace; the bouquet had fallen to the floor, and presently the submissive victim stood with only chemise and drawers. What a glimpse I had of her splendid white neck and bosom, what deliciously full and rounded legs, with pink silk stockings and handsome garters (for the General was very strict as to the costume of his penitents).

I assisted to tie her up, and unfastening her drawers, Jane drew them well down, whilst Mrs. Mansell pinned up her chemise, fully exposing the broad expanse of her glorious buttocks, the brilliant whiteness of her skin showing to perfection by the dazzling glare of the well-lighted room. I gave her two or three smart pats of approval just to let her know I hadn't forgotten the slap she gave me, then drew aside to make way for Sir Eyre.

My thoughts were so entirely absorbed by the fascinating spectacle that I lost all remembrance of my own impending turn. Whack! came the big birch, with a force to have made her jump out of her skin, if possible, but only a stifled, "Ah-r-r-re!" and a broad, red mark were the results; the blood mounted to her face, and she seemed to hold her breath for each blow as it came, but the rod was so heavy, and the old General so vigorous, that in less than a dozen strokes her fair bottom was smeared with blood and bits of birch were lying in all directions. "Ah! Ah!! Oh!!!" she screamed, "do have mercy, sir, I can't stand it. Oh! oh! indeed I can't."

"You sly thief, don't think I'll let you off before you're dead; if I don't cure you now I shall lose a good servant," exclaimed Sir Eyre, cutting away.

My blood boiled with excitement of a most pleasurable kind, young as I was, and cruel as I knew it to be, no pity for the victim entered my breast; it is a sensation only to be experienced by real lovers of the rod.

"You like rum, do you, Miss?" said the General. "Did you take it raw or mixed? I'll make your bottom raw."

The poor old man was obliged now to sit down for want of breath, Mrs. Mansell, understanding his wishes, at once took his place with a fresh birch, without giving the victim any respite.

"She must, indeed, be well punished, sir. I'm sure they're never denied anything so long as they behave themselves," said she, with a stern relentless face; in fact, after a stroke or two, her light-brown hair was all in disorder from the exertion, and her dashing hazel eyes, and well-turned figure, made me think her a goddess of vengeance.

"Will you? Will you do so again? You ungrateful thief," she kept on saying, with a blow to each question.

Poor Jemima moaned, sobbed, and sometimes cried out for mercy, whilst the blood fairly trickled down her thighs, but the housekeeper seemed to hear nothing and Sir Evre was in an ecstasy of gloating delight. This could not last long, however strong the victim might be. Becoming exhausted, with her accumulated sensations, she at last fairly fainted, and we had to dash cold water over her face to recover her; then covered with a cloak, she was led off to her room, and left to herself.

"Now, Rosa," said the General, holding out a light green bunch of fresh birch, "kiss the rod, and get ready for your turn."

Hardly knowing what I was about, I inclined my head and gave the required kiss, Mrs. Mansell and Jane had me prepared in no time, as I was quite passive; and as soon as I was fairly exposed and spread-eagled on the horse, the old General rose to his task.

"You have seen how severe I can be, by Jemima's punishment," said he; "but, perhaps, you did not think your answer to me yesterday was any offense, and I am almost inclined toforgive you, but remember in future, if you get off lightly this time, a plain lie is better than prevarication. I think the last flogging must have done you great good, your conduct is quite different tonight. But now, remember-remember- remember!" he cried again, giving sharp, cutting strokes at each word. My poor bottom tingled with agony, and I cried loudly for mercy, promising to be strictly truthful in future; so, after about twenty strokes, he said: "You may go this time," finishing me off with a tremendous remembrance, which made me fairly shake with the concussion, and was the only blow which actually drew the blood, although I had some fine tender weals. This must finish my second letter. Believe me my true-bom child of the rod,

Your loving friend,

ROSA BELINDA COOTE.

(To be continued.)

LADY POKINGHAM, OR THEY ALL DO IT

Giving an Account of her Luxurious Adventures, both before and after her Marriage with Lord Crim-Con.

*

Part I

(Continued.)

William felt ready to drop; the perspiration stood on his brow in great drops, but his lips refused to speak, and Alice continued in a soft whisper: "I saw it all this morning, Willie dear, and what joy that great red-head thing of yours seemed to give her. You must let me into the secret, and I will never tell. This is the monster you shoved into her so furiously. I must look at it and feel it; how hard it has got under my touch. La! What a funny thing! I can get it out as Lucy did," pulling open his trousers and letting out the rampant engine of love. She kissed its red velvety head, saying: "What a sweet, soft thing to touch. Oh! I must caress it a little." Her touches were like fire to his senses; speechless with rapture and surprise, he silently submitted to the freak of the wilful girl, but his novel position was so exciting, he could not restrain himself, but the sperm boiled up from his penis all over her hands and face.

"Ah!" she exclaimed. "That's just what I saw it do yesterday morning. Does it do that inside of Lucy?"

Here William recovered himself a little, and wiping her face and hands with his handkerchief, put away the rude plaything, saying,

"Oh! My God! I'm lost! What have you done, Alice? It's awful! Never mention it again. I mustn't walk out with you any more."

Alice burst into sobs.

"Oh! Oh! Willie! How unkind! Do you think I will tell? Only I must share the pleasure with Lucy. Oh! Kiss me as you did her, and we won't say any more about it to-day."

William loved the little girl too well to refuse such a delightful task, but he contented himself with a very short suck at her virgin cunny, lest his erotic passion should urge him to outrage her at once.

"How nice to feel your lovely tongue there. How beautifully it tickled and warmed me all over; but you were so quick, and left off just as it seemed nicer than ever, dear Willie," said Alice, embracing and kissing him with ardour,

"Gently, darling; you mustn't be so impulsive; it's a very dangerous game for one so young. You must be careful how you look at me, or notice me, before others," said Mr. William, returning her kisses, and feeling himself already quite unable to withstand the temptation of such a delicious liaison.

"Ah!" said Alice, with extraordinary perception for one so young. "You fear Lucy. Our best plan is to take her into our , confidence. I will get rid of my lady's-maid, I never did like her, and will ask mama to give Lucy the place. Won't that be fine, dear? We shall be quite safe in all our little games then."

The butler, now more collected in his ideas, and with a cooler brain, could not but admire the wisdom of this arrangement, so he assented to the plan, and he took the boat put for a row to cool their heated blood, and quiet the impulsive throbbings of a pair of fluttering hearts.

The next two or three days were wet and unfavourable for outdoor excursions, and Alice took advantage of this interval to induce her mother to change her lady's-maid, and install Lucy in the situation.

Alice's attendant slept in a little chamber, which had two doors, one opening into the corridor, whilst the other allowed free and direct access to her little mistress's apartment, which it adjoined.

The very first night Lucy retired to rest in her new room, she had scarcely been half-an-hour in bed (where she lay, reflecting on the change, and wondering how she would now be able to enjoy the butler's company occasionally), before Alice called out for her. In a moment she was at the young lady's bedside, saying: "What can I do, Miss Alice, are you not warm enough? These damp nights are so chilly."

"Yes, Lucy," said Alice, "that must be what it is. I feel cold and restless. Would you mind getting in bed with me? You will soon make me warm."

Lucy jumped in, and Alice nestled close up to her bosom, as if for warmth, but in reality to feel the outlines of her beautiful figure.

"Kiss me, Lucy," she said; "I know I shall like you so much better than Mary. I couldn't bear her." This was lovingly responded to, and Alice continued, as she pressed her hand on the bosom of her bedfellow, "What large titties you have, Lucy. Let me feel them. Open your nightdress, so I can lay my face against them."

The new femme de chambre was naturally of a warm and loving disposition; she admitted all the familiarities of her young mistress, whose hands began to wander in a most searching manner about her person, feeling the soft, firm skin of her bosom, belly, and bottom; the touches of Alice seemed to fire the blood, and rouse every voluptuous emotion within her; she sighed and kissed her little mistress again and again.

ALICE.-"What a fine rump! How hard and plump your flesh is, Lucy! Oh, my! what's all this hair at the bottom of your belly? My dear, when did it come?"

LUCY.-"Oh! pray don't, Miss, it's so rude; you will be the same in two or three years' time; it frightened me when it first began to grow, it seemed so unnatural."

ALICE.-"We're only girls, there is no harm in touching each other, is there; just feel how different I am."

LUCY.-"Oh! Miss Alice," pressing the young girl's naked belly to her own, "you don't know how you make me feel when you touch me there."

ALICE (with a slight laugh).-"Does it make you feel better when Mr. William, the butler, touches you, dear?" tickling the hairy crack with her finger.

LUCY.-"For shame, Miss! I hope you don't think I would let him touch me"; evidently in some confusion.

ALICE.-"Don't be frightened, Lucy, I won't tell, but I have seen it all through the old glass door in his pantry. Ah! you see I know the secret, and must be let in to share the fun."

LUCY.-"Oh! My God! Miss Alice, what have you seen? I shall have to leave the house at once."

ALICE.-"Come, come, don't be frightened, you know I'm fond of Mr. William, and would never do him any harm, but you can't have him all to yourself; I got you for my maid to prevent your jealous suspicions and keep our secret between us."

Lucy was in a frightful state of agitation. "What! has he been such a brute as to ruin you, Miss Alice! I'll murder him if he has," she cried.

ALICE.-"Softly, Lucy, not so loud, someone will hear you; he's done nothing yet, but I saw your pleasure when he put that thing into your crack, and am determined to share your joys, so don't be jealous, and we can all three be happy together."

LUCY.-"It would kill you dear; that big thing of his would split you right up."

ALICE.-"Never mind," kissing her lovingly, "you keep the secret and I'm not afraid of being seriously hurt."

Lucy sealed the compact with a kiss, and they spent a most loving night together, indulging in every variety of kissing and tickling, and Alice had learnt from her bedfellow nearly all the mysterious particulars in connection with the battles of Venus before they fell asleep in each other's arms.

Fine weather soon returned, and Alice, escorted by the butler, went for one of her usual rambles, and they soon penetrated into a thick copse at the further end of the park, and sat down in a little grassy spot, where they were secure from observation.

William had thoughtfully brought with him an umbrella, as well as a great coat and cloak, which he spread upon the grass for fear Miss Alice might take cold.

"Ah! you dear old fellow," said Alice, seating herself, and, taking his hand, pulled him down beside her. "I understand everything now, and you are to make me happy by making a woman of me, as you did Lucy; you must do it, Willie, dear, I shall soon make you so you can't help yourself." Unbuttoning his trousers and handling his already stiff pego, "What a lovely dear it is; how I long to feel its juice spouting into my bowels; I know it's painful, but it won't kill me, and then, ah! the heavenly bliss I know you will make me feel, as you do Lucy when you have her; how will you do it? Will you lay over me?"

William, unable to resist her caresses and already almost at spending point, makes her kneel over his face, as he lay on his back, so that he may first lubricate her maiden cunny with his tongue. This operation titillates and excites the little girl, so that she amorously presses herself on his mouth as she faces towards his cock, which she never leaves hold of all the while; he spends in ecstasy, whilst she also feels the pleasure of a first virgin emission.

"Now's the time, Alice, dear, my affair is so well greased, and your pussey is also ready; if I get over you I might be too violent and injure you; the best way is for you to try and do it yourself by straddling over me, and directing its bead to your cunny, and then keep pressing down upon it, as well as the first painful sensations will allow; it will all depend on your own courage for the success of the experiment," said William,

ALICE.-"Ah! you shall see my determination," as she began to act upon his suggestion, and fitting the bead of his pego into her slit, soon pressed down so as to take in and quite cover the first inch of it.

Here the pain of stretching and distension seemed almost too much for her, but she gave a sudden downward plunge of her body, which, although she almost fainted with the dreadful pain, got in at least three inches.

"What a plucky girl you are, my dear Alice," said William, in delight. "As soon as you can bear it, raise yourself up a little, and come down with all your force. It is so well planted, the next good thrust will complete my possession of your lovely charms."

"I don't care if I die in the effort," she whispered, softly."Never mind how it hurts me, help all you can, Willie dear,this time," as she raised herself off him again, and he tookhold of her buttocks, to lend his assistance to the grave girl.

Clenching her teeth firmly, and shutting her eyes, she gave another desperate plunge upon William's spear of love, the hymen was broken, and she was fairly impaled to the roots of his affair. But it cost her dear, she fell forward in a dead faint, whilst the trickling blood proved the sanguinary nature of Love's victory.

The butler withdrew himself, all smeared with her virgin blood, but he had come prepared for such an emergency, and at once set about using restoratives to bring her round, and presently succeeded in his efforts; her eyes opened with a smile, and whispering softly, Alice said:-

"Ah! that last thrust was awful, but it's over now. Why did you take him away? Oh! put it back at once, dear, and let me have the soothing injection Lucy said would soon heal all my bruised parts."

He glued his lips to hers, and gently applied the head of his pego to her blood-stained crack, gradually inserted it till it was three-fourths in; then, without pressing further, he commenced to move slowly and carefully. The lubricity soon increased, and he could feel the tight loving contractions of her vagina, which speedily brought him to a crisis once more, and with a sudden thrust, he plunged up to the hilt, and shot his very essence into her bowels, as he almost fainted with the excess of his emotions.

They laid motionless, enjoying each other's mutual pressures, till Mr. William withdrew, and taking a fine cambric handkerchief, wiped the virgin blood first from the lips of her cunny, then off his own weapon, declaring, as he put the red-stained mouchoir in his pocket, that he would keep it for ever, in remembrance of the charms she had so lovingly surrendered to him.

The butler prudently refrained from the further indulgence in voluptuous pleasure for the day, and, after a good rest, Alice returned to the house, feeling very little the worse for her sacrifice, and very happy in having secured part of the love of dear and faithful William.

How suddenly unforeseen accidents prevent the realization of the best plans for happiness. The very same day, her father was ordered by his medical adviser to the South of Europe, and started next morning for town, to make the necessary arrangements, taking the butler with him, leaving Alice's mama to follow as soon as the two children were suitably located at school.

Lucy and her young mistress consoled each other as well as possible under the circumstances. But in a few days, an aunt took charge of the house, and Alice was sent to this school, and is now in your arms, dear Beatrice; whilst my brother is now at college, and we only meet during the holidays. Will you, dear, ask your guardians to allow you to spend the next vacation with me, and I will introduce you to Frederick, who, if I make no mistake, is quite as voluptuously inclined as his sister.

Part II

I will pass over the exciting practices myself and bed-fellow used to indulge in almost every night, and merely remark that two more finished young tribades it would have been impossible to have found anywhere.

I had to wait till the Christmas vacation before I could be introduced to Frederick, who, between ourselves, we had already devoted to the task of taking my virginity, which we did not think would prove a very difficult operation, as with so much finger frigging, and also the use of Alice's leather sausage, which, as I learnt, she had improvised for her own gratification, my mount and cunny were wonderfully developed, and already slight signs of the future growth of curly brown hair could be detected. It was one fine crisp morning in December we drove up to the Hall on our return from school. There stood the aunt to welcome us, but my eyes were fixed upon the youthful, yet manly figure of Frederick, who stood by her side, almost a counterpart of his sister, in features and complexion, but really a very fine young fellow, of not much more than eighteen.

Since hearing the story of Alice's intrigue with William, I always looked at every man and boy to see what sort of a bunch they had got in their pockets, and was delighted to perceive Mr. Frederick was apparently well furnished.

Alice introduced me to her relatives, but Frederick evidently looked upon me as a little girl, and not at all yet up to the serious business of love and flirtation, so our first private consultation, between Alice and myself, was how best to open his eyes, and draw him to take a little more notice of his sister's friend.

Lucy, who I now saw for the first time, slept in the little room adjoining Alice's chamber, which I shared with her young mistress. Frederick had a room on the other side of ours, so that we were next door neighbours, and could rap and give signals to each other on the wall, as well as to try to look through the keyhole of a disused door, which opened direct from one room to the other, but had long since been locked and bolted to prevent any communication between the occupants.

A little observation soon convinced us that Lucy was upon most intimate terms with her young master, which Alice determined to turn to account in our favour.

She quickly convinced her femme de chambre that she could not enjoy and monopolize the whole of her brother, and finding that Lucy expected he would visit her room that very night, she insisted upon ringing the changes, by taking Lucy to sleep with herself, and putting me in the place of Monsieur Frederick's ladylove.

I was only too willing to be a party of this arrangement, and at ten P.M., when we all retired to rest, I took the place of the femme de chambre, and pretended to be fast asleep in her snug little bed. The lock of the door had been oiled by Lucy, so as to open quite noiselessly, but the room was purposely left in utter darkness, and secured even from the intrusion of a dim starlight by well-closed window curtains.

About eleven o'clock, as nearly as I could guess, the door silently opened, and by the light of the corridor lamp, I saw a figure, in nothing but a shirt, cautiously glide in, and approach the bed. The door closed, and all was dark, putting my heart in a dreadful flutter, at the approach of the long wished for, but dreaded ravisher of my virginity.

"Lucy! Lucy!! Lucy!!!" he whispered, in a low voice, almost in my ear. No response, only the apparent deep breathing of a person in sound sleep.

"She hasn't thought much about me, but, I guess, something between her legs will soon wake her up," I heard him mutter; then the bedclothes were pulled open, and he slid into bed by my side. My hair was all loose, the same as Lucy's generally was at night, and I felt a warm kiss on my cheek, also an arm stealing round my waist and clutching my nightdress as if to pull it up. Of course I was the fox asleep, but could not help being all atremble at the approach of my fate.

"How you shake, Lucy; what's the matter? Hullo! who's this; it can't be you?" he said rapidly, as with a sigh and a murmur, "Oh! Oh! Alice." I turned round just as he pulled up my chemise, clasping my arm firmly round him, but still apparently lost in sleep. "My God!" I heard him say, "It's that little devil of a Beatrice in Lucy's bed; I won't go, I'll have a lark, she can't know me in the dark."

His hands seemed to explore every part of my body; I could feel his rampant cock pressed between our naked bellies, but although in a burning heat of excitement, I determined to let him do just as he liked, and pretend still to be asleep; his fingers explored my crack, and rubbed the little clitoris; first his leg got between mine, and then presently I could feel him gently placing the head of his instrument in the crack, and I was so excited that a sudden emission wetted it and his fingers all over with a creamy spend. "The little devil's spending in her sleep; these girls must be in the habit of frigging each other, I believe," he said to himself again. Then his lips met mine for the first time, and he was quite free from fear on that account as his face was as beardless as a girl's.

"Ah! Alice!" I murmured, "give me your sausage thing, that's it, dear, shove it in," as I pushed myself forward on his slowly progressing cock; he met me with a sudden thrust, making me almost scream with pain, yet my arms nervously clung round his body, and kept him close to the mark.

"Gently," he whispered, "Beatrice, dear, I'm Frederick, I won't hurt you much; how in heaven's name did you come in Lucy's bed?"

Pretending now to awaken for the first time with a little scream, and trying to push his body away from me, I exclaimed, "Oh! Oh! How you hurt! Oh! for shame, don't. Oh! let me go, Mr. Frederick, how can you?" And then my efforts seemed exhausted, and I lay almost at his mercy as he ruthlessly pushed his advantage, and tried to stop my mouth with kisses. I was lost. Although very painful, thanks to our frequent fingerings, etc., the way had been so cleared that he was soon in complete possession, although as I afterwards found by the stains on my chemise it was not quite a bloodless victory.

Taking every possible advantage, he continued his motions with thrilling energy, till I could not help responding to his delicious thrusts, moving my bottom a little to meet each returning insertion of his exciting weapon (we were lying on our sides), and in a few moments we both swam in a mutual flood of bliss, and after a spasmodic storm of sighs, kisses, and tender hugging pressure of each other's body, we lay in a listless state of enjoyment, when suddenly the bedclothes were thrown, or pulled off, then slap-slap-slap, came smarting smacks on our bottoms, and Alice's light, merry laugh sounded through the darkness, "Ha! Ha! Ha! Ha! Mr. Frederick, is this what you learnt at college, sir? Here, Lucy, help; we must secure and punish the wretch; bring a light."

Lucy appeared with a candle and locked the door inside at once, before he could have a chance of escaping, and I could see she was quite delighted at the spectacle presented by our bodies in conjunction, for as I had been previously instructed, I clung to him in apparent fright, and tried to hide my blushing face in his bosom.

Frederick was in the utmost confusion, and at first was afraid his sister would expose him, but he was a little re-assured as she went on, "What shall I do? I can't tell an old maid like aunt; only to think that my dear little Beatrice should be outraged under my very eyes, the second night of her visit. If papa and mama were at home, they would know what to do; now I must decide for myself.

Now, Frederick, will you submit to a good whipping for this, or shall I write to your father, and send Beatrice home disgraced in the morning, and you will have to promise to marry her, sir? Now you've spoilt her for anyone else; who do you think would take a cruche cassée if they knew it, or not repudiate her when it was found out, as it must be the first night of her marriage. No, you bad boy, I'm determined both to punish you and make you offer her all the reparation in your power."

I began to cry, and begged her not to be too hard, as he had not hurt me much, and in fact had, at the finish, quite delighted my ravished senses.

"Upon my word," said Alice, assuming the airs of a woman, "the girl is as bad as the boy; this could not have happened, Beatrice, if you had not been too complaisant, and given way to his rudeness."

Frederick, disengaging himself from my embrace, and quite unmindful of his condition, started up, and clasping his sister round her neck, kissed her most lovingly, and the impudent fellow even raised her nightdress and stroked her belly, exclaiming, as he passed his hand over her mossy mount, "What a pity, Alice, you are my sister or I would give you the same pleasure as I have Beatrice, but I will submit to your chastisement, however hard it may be, and promise also that my little love here shall be my future wife."

ALICE.-"You scandalous fellow, to insult my modesty so, and expose your blood-stained manhood to my sight, but I will punish you, and avenge both myself and Beatrice; you are my prisoner, so just march into the other room, I've got a tickler there that I brought home from school, as a curiosity, little thinking I should so soon have a use for it."

Arrived in Alice's own room, she and Lucy first tied his hands to the bedpost, then they secured his ankles to the handle of a heavy box, which stood handy, so as to have him tolerably well stretched out.

ALICE, getting her rod out of a drawer.-"Now, pin up his shirt to his shoulders, and I will see if I can't at least draw a few drops of his impudent blood out of his posteriors, which Beatrice may wipe off with her handkerchief as a memento of the outrage she has so easily forgiven."

The hall was a large house, and our apartments were the only ones occupied in that corridor, the rooms abutting on which were all in reserve for visitors expected to arrive in a few days, to spend Christmas with us, so that there was not much fear of being heard by any of the other inmates of the house, and Alice was under no necessity of thinking what might be the result of her blows. With a flourish she brought down the bunch of twigs with a thundering whack on his plump, white bottom; the effect was startling to the culprit, who was evidently only anticipating some playful fun. "Ah! My God! Alice, you'll cut the skin; mind what you're about; I didn't bargain for that."

ALICE (with a smile of satisfaction).-"Ho! Ho! did you think I was going to play with you? But, you've soon found your mistake, sir. Will you? Will you, again take such outrageous liberties with a young lady friend of mine?"

She cut him quite half-a-dozen times in rapid succession, as she thus lectured him, each blow leaving long red lines, to mark its visitation, and suffusing his fair bottom all over with a peach-like bloom. The victim, finding himself quite helpless, bit his lips and ground his teeth in fruitless rage. At last he burst forth: "Ah! Ah! You she-devil! Do you mean to skin my bum? Be careful, or I will take a rare revenge some day before long."

ALICE, with great calmness and determination, but with a most excited twinkle in her eyes.-"Oh! You show temper, do you? So you mean to be revenged on me for doing a simple act of justice, sir? I will keep you there, and cut away at your impudent bottom, till you fairly beg my pardon, and promise to forgo all such wicked revengefulness."

The victim writhed in agony and rage, but her blows only increased in force, beginning to raise great fiery-looking weals all over his buttocks. "Ah! Ha!" she continued, "How do you like it, Fred? Shall I put a little more steam in my blows?"

Frederick struggles desperately to get loose, but they have secured him too well for that! The tears of shame and mortification stand in his eyes, but he is still obstinate, and I could also observe a very perceptible rising in his manly instrument, which soon stood out from his belly in a rampant state of erection.

ALICE, with assumed fury.-"Look at the fellow, how he is insulting me, by the exhibition of his lustful weapon. I wish I could cut it off with a blow of the rod," giving him a fearful cut across his belly and on the penis.

Frederick fairly howled with pain, and big tears rolled down his cheeks, as he gasped out: "Oh! Oh! Ah! Have mercy, Alice. I know I deserve it. Oh! Pity me now, dear!"

ALICE, without relaxing her blows.-"Oh! You are beginning to feel properly, are you? Are you sincerely penitent? Beg my pardon at once, sir, for the way you insulted me in the other room."

FREDERICK.-"Oh! Dear Alice! Stop! Stop! You don't let me get any breath. I will! I will beg your pardon. Oh! I can't help my affair sticking up as it does."

ALICE.-"Down sir! Down sir! Your master is ashamed of you," as she playfully whisks his pego with her rod.

Frederick is in agony; his writhing and contortions seemed

excruciating in the extreme, he fairly groaned out: "Oh! Oh! Alice, let me down. On my word, I will do anything you order. Oh! Oh! Ah! You make me do it," as he shuts his eyes, and we saw quite a jet of sperm shoot from his virile member.

Alice dropped her rod, and we let down the culprit who was terribly crestfallen.

"Now, sir," she said, "down on your knees, and kiss the rod."

Without a word, he dropped down, and kissed the worn out stump, saying: "Oh! Alice; the last few moments have been so heavenly. It has blotted out all sense of pain. My dear sister, I thank you for punishing me, and will keep my promise to Beatrice."

I wiped the drops of blood from his slightly-bleeding rump, and then we gave him a couple of glasses of wine, and allowed him to sleep with Lucy, in her room, for the rest of the night, where they had a most luscious time of it, whilst Alice and myself indulged in our favourite touches.

You may be sure Frederick was not long before he renewed his pleasures with me, whilst his sister took pleasure in our happiness; but she seemed to have contracted a penchant for the use of the rod, and, once or twice a week, would have us all in her room, for a birch seance, as she called it, when Lucy or myself had to submit to be victims; but the heating of our bottoms only seemed to add to our enjoyment when we were afterwards allowed to soothe our raging passions in the arms of our mutual lover.

(To be continued.)

INTERLUDE

A gentleman, who is blessed with a beautiful and lewdly disposed wife, has long been very unhappy and disappointed at the results of his endeavours to become a parent. But returning home from the City, very unexpectedly, the other morning, he caught the Vicar of the parish gamahuching his spouse. "Ho! Ho!" he exclaimed, in a fury. "So you're the bugger who swallows all my children."

PART OF A LETTER FROM HARRIET KEENE

I'll tell you a funny dream I had the night before last. I thought I was sitting on a green bank, and a man was sitting by the side of me; he fell to kissing and talking, but did nothing else. Well, after a while, he got up and went away; then, at the side of me, as I sat there, lay the largest prick I ever saw. It was at least half a yard long, and as thick as the calf of my leg; it had four bollox, but it tapered towards the end. I thought I took it up and felt it. It was warm flesh and blood, and I said to myself, "Why the man has left his prick behind him; what a pity! and it is such a fine one tool what will he do without it?" So I thought to myself, "I wonder if it will spend if I suck it," so I kept sucking it, but it was so big and thick that it made my mouth ache, and I said to myself, "Never mind, it will do to frig myself with." So I got up, and put it under my cloak, and cuddled it so close to me that I felt as lewd as could be. As I was going along I met the man coming back, and when he came up to me, he said, "Have you seen my trumpet?" "Your trumpet," said I, "why you mean your prick!" Says he, "You nasty, lying woman, it's my best trumpet." "Well," said I, "if this is a trumpet, why a trumpet's a prick, and a prick is a trumpet," and I held it up to look at. He snatched it out of my hand. "Now, then, I'll show you if it's a prick or a trumpet," and he began to blow away on it so loud that I awoke and lost my prick and trumpet too.

What woke me up was the sound of a trumpet in the street, so I suppose that was the cause of my funny dream.

THE WISE LOVER

Woman and man whene'er inclined,
In mutual goodness pleasure find,
The lawful spouse 'tis sweet to embrace,
In hopes to see a lengthen'd race,
But let who will the truth contest,
Another's wife is still the best.

When I was young and slightly skill'd,
In blisses womankind can yield;
I lov'd the maid, I lov'd the piece;
But as my wit and years increase,
I own the sweetest sport in life,
Is to enjoy your neighbour's wife.

A virgin coy with sidelong eye,
Your mere approach, at once will fly,
Abhors your nasty hot desires,
Nought less than marriage she requires,
Such maidenheads the wise detest,
The adultery maidenhead's the best.

The vagrant nymph who sells her charms,
And fills in turn a thousand arms,
Besides the loss of gold and fame,
May set Priapus in a flame,

Such fire-tailed comets God confound.
A wife is always safe and sound.

The genial flame I've oft allayed,
With buxom Kate, my chambermaid,
And dozens such as her, but found
Such sport with ills beset around;
He who at liberty would feast,
Will find another's wife the best.

A mistress kept at first is sweet,
And joys to do the merry feat;
But bastards come, and hundreds gone,
You'll wish you'd left her charms alone;
Such breeding hussy's are a pest,
A neighbour's wife is far the best.
If you are rash, a wife at first
May into horrid fury burst,
"Sir, you shall rue throughout your life
The day you've kissed another's wife."
Reply, "My dear, this gives the zest,
I always like my neighbour's best."

Jove, I remember, when inclined
To feast himself on womankind,
Though maids enough to him were free,
Always preferr'd adultery;
He took the shape of bird and beast,
To prove Adultery the best.

But while this naughty sport we sing,
Who can forget our gracious King (Geo. IV);
Him many a lady pleasures gives,
For which her husband pay receives,
God bless King George! His Majesty
Is patron of Adultery.

I own the dangers of the suit,

The sweetest is forbidden fruit,
And laws as thick as hairs are set,
Around the center of delight;
This peril gives the highest zest,
And guarded hoard is sure the best.

The wandering nymph your purse desires,
The chambermaid to rank aspires;
Your wife content with marriage dues,
All further license will refuse;
He who has put them to the test,
Must own his neighbour's wife's the best.

QUEEN BATHSHEBA

*

A Temperance Ballad. (Attributed to Sir Wilfrid Lawson.)

Grass widows and princes! a warning I sing,
Of the sad wicked doing of David, the King;
With Bathsheba, wife of poor Major Uriah,
Who was bathing one day, when the King chanc'd to spy her.

He was drinking up-stairs, and the weather was hot;
And her window was open (a thing she forgot);
And the stark-naked beauty had not an idea,
That while she was washing, a creature could see her!

She and her little sister were sporting together,
Enjoying the heat of the bright summer weather;
They bath'd in the fountain, and while they were washing,
Were romping all naked, and leaping and splashing.

What man could resist such an awful temptation?
He forgot he was King of the sanctified nation;
He was fill'd with delight, and lewd admiration,
And was mad for the raptures of fierce fornication.

Beware of the Devil, who seldom lies sleeping!
So while she was washing, and while he was peeping,

The King's living sceptre grew stiff as a rod,
"Nice mutton!" cried David, "I'll fuck her, by G-!"

So calling a page, he desir'd him to go,
And enquire all about her.-He answered, "I know
The lady your Majesty's pleas'd to admire,
Is the wife of the valorous Major Uriah."

His Majesty answer'd: "Go, fetch her! Be quick!
Much conscience, indeed, has a stiff-standing prick!"
The page ran to call her; she put on her smock,
And hurried to wait on his Majesty's cock.

One touch to her hand, and one word in her ear,
And she fell on her back, like a sweet willing dear;
He was frantic with lust, but she seiz'd his erection,
And put it at once in the proper direction.

She was girlish and lively, a heavenly figure,
With the cunt of an angel, and fucking with vigour;
He got her at once with child of a son,
And he said a long grace when the swiving was done.

So the lady went home, and she very soon found
Her belly was growing unluckily round.
"This an honour," said she, "I could hardly expect,
Your Majesty now must your handmaid protect."

"Never fear," cried the King, "I'll be your adviser,
I'll send for the Major, and no one's the wiser."
So he sent for Uriah, who speedily came.
But unluckily never laid hands on the dame.

King David was puzzled, he made the man tipsy,
But still he avoided the lewd little gipsy;
David laid a new plot, and his wish was fulfill'd,
In the front of the battle Uriah was kill'd.

THE HORRIBLE FRIGHT

Poor Sally! I hear from your loving Mamma,
That you're in a horrible fright of Papa;
Take courage, dear girl, for the sweetest delight,
Is closely akin to a horrible fright.

In your dreams, did you ne'er see a horrible man,
Who crushes and conquers you, do all you can?
He treats your poor innocent mouse like a rat
That's touzled and claw'd, and devour'd by a cat.

He produces a horrible fright of a thing,
That fits like a finger in conjugal ring;
He thrusts, and he pokes, and he enters your belly,
Till the horrible monster is melted to jelly.

When you draw a new glove on your finger so tight,
The glove is, you know, in a horrible fright;
But soon it is taught your dear finger to love,
The man and the woman are finger and glove.

Away with your horrible fright, and away
With the wretch of a father, who hinders the play;
If he dares interfere, when you kiss on the sly,
Just pull up your petticoat, piss in his eye.

Ah! Sally, my darling, I wish that this night,
I might put you, my love, in a horrible fright;
You might lie down a maiden, in five minutes more,
I would open a secret, ne'er open'd before.

You then would behold, long, ruddy, and thick,
That horrible monster, a stiff-standing prick;
You'd cry out, "Oh, softly! Oh, gently! Ah! Ah!
Oh lordy, oh lordy, oh harder, la! la!"

At last, dearest Sally, your horrible fright
Would end in a shudder of tipsy delight;
You'll open your buttocks, as wide as you can,
To admit every inch of the dear cruel man.

You'll devour every inch of his horrible yard,
Till the testicles hit on your bottom so hard;
Your terrible fright, my dear girl, will be over,
You'll breathe out your soul, on the lips of your lover.

There's an end of this horrible fright of a song,
Your mother shall read it, and say if it's wrong;
No, she will approve it-her greatest delight
Is the prick which you fancy such a horrible fright.

PAYNE'S HILL (Mons Veneris)

In Middlesex a hill we meet,
For beauty known to fame;
Where wealthy Payne has built his seat,
Payne's Hill they call its name.

"Pray, Mr. Burke," said Lady Payne,
"What Latin word is this?
(I've searched the dictionary in vain),
Pray what's Mons Veneris?"

He look'd into her beauteous eyes,
So innocent of ill;
And gave the happiest of replies,
"It signifies Payne's Hill!"

INSTANCE OF SELF-DENIAL

Mohammed Sadig, a gentleman at Hyderabad, received a female slave, belonging to his brother at Kurnool, who was going to Bengal, and requested Sadig to keep his property for a year. Her beauty excited his passions greatly. He told the story to my friend, Captain Keighley, and ended thus: "To lie with her carnally would have been wrong, as my brother had not permitted it, so I governed my love by the holy rules of moderation and virtue, and contented myself with merely fucking her in the arse."

George Stokes, the cheesemonger in Snowhill, had Dr. Cullen one night as a guest. Cullen did not fancy the cheese on the table, and said, "You do not know how to select cheese; let me go into the warehouse and pick one out." He did this, and the cheese he selected was delicious. Everyone declared it most excellent. "How did you pitch upon it, and in the dark, too?" said Stokes. "I'll tell you," said the Doctor. "I tried several, till I came to one which made my prick stand. This is it; a prime cheese smells exactly like a blooming, ripe, girl's cunt."

NURSERY RHYMES

There was a young lady of Gaza,
Who shaved her cunt dean with a razor;
The crabs in a lump
Made tracks to her rump,
Which proceeding did greatly amaze her.

There was a young lass of Surat,
The cheeks of whose arse were so fat
That they had to be parted,
Whenever she farted,
And also whenever she shat.

There was an old priest of Siberia,
Who of fucking grew wearier and wearier;
So one night after prayers,
He bolted upstairs,
And buggered the Lady Superior.

There was an old man of Natal,
Who was lazily fucking a gal,
Says she, "You're a sluggard,"
Said he, "You be buggered,
I like to fuck slowly, and shall."

There was a young farmer of Nant;

Whose conduct was gay and gallant,
For he fucked all his dozens
Of nieces and cousins,
In addition, of course, to his aunt.

There was an old man of Tantivy,
Who followed his son to the privy,
He lifted the lid,
To see what he did,
And found that it smelt of Capivi.

There was a young man of this Nation,
Who didn't much like fornication;
When asked, "Do you fuck?"
He said, "No, I suck Women's quims,
and I use Masturbation."

There was a young parson of Eltham,
Who seldom fucked whores, but oft felt 'em.
In the lanes he would linger,
And play at stick finger,
'Twas on the way home that he smelt 'em.

There was a young lady of Rheims,
Who was terribly plagued with wet dreams;
She saved up a dozen,
And sent to her cousin,
Who ate them and thought they were creams.

There was a gay parson of Tooting,
Whose roe he was frequently shooting;
Till he married a lass,
With a face like my arse,
And a cunt you could put a top-boot in.

A learned divine down at Buckingham,
Wrote a treatise on cunts and on fucking 'em;
A learned Parsee,

Taught him Gamahuchee,
So he added a chapter on sucking 'em.

NOT THE THING

Said Lady Macneill,to Sir John, eating ling,
I'm afraid. Sir, that fish ain't exactly the thing
Why really, he answer'd, I do not dislike it,
It's not the thing, but it's mightily like it.

VOLUME III

* * * * *

Published Monthly

Sept. 1879

SUB-UMBRA, OR SPORT AMONG THE SHE-NOODLES

(continued)

In the course of the evening, Frank and myself were delighted by the arrival of a beautiful young lady, on a visit to his sisters, in fact, a school fellow of Sophie and Polly, come to stop a week at the house.

Miss Rosa Redquim was indeed a sprightly beauty of the Venus height, well proportioned in leg and limb, full swelling bosom, with a graceful Grecian type of face, rosy cheeks, large grey eyes, and golden auburn hair, lips as red as cherries, and teeth like pearls, frequently exhibited by a succession of winning smiles, which never seemed to leave her face. Such was the acquisition to the feminine department of the house, and we congratulated ourselves on the increased prospect of sport, as Frank had expressed to me considerable compunctions as to taking liberties with one's own sisters.

The next morning being gloriously fine and warm, myself and friend strolled in the grounds, smoking our cigarettes, for about an hour, till near the time when we guessed the girls would be coming for a bath in the small lake in the park, which we at once proceeded to; then we secreted ourselves secure from observation, and awaited, in deep silence, the arrival of sisters and friend.

This lake, as I call it, was a pond of about four or five acres in extent, every side thickly wooded to the very margin, so that even anglers could not get access to the bank, except at the little sloping green sward, of about twenty or thirty square yards in extent, which had a large hut, or summer-house, under the trees, where the bathers could undress, and then trip across the lawn to the water. The bottom of the pond being gradually shelving, and covered with fine sand at this spot, and a circular space, enclosed with rails, to prevent them getting out of their depth.

The back door of this hut opened upon a very narrow foot-path, leading to the house through the dense thicket, so that any party would feel quite secure from observation. The interior was comfortably furnished with seats and lounges, besides a buffet, generally holding a stock of wine, biscuits, and cakes, during the bathing season.

Frank, having a key to the hut, took me through onto the lawn, and then climbing up into a thick sycamore, we re-lighted our cigarettes, awaiting the adventure with some justifiable impatience.

Some ten minutes of suspense, and then we were rewarded by hearing the ringing laughter of the approaching girls. We heard the key turned in the lock, then the sounds of their bolting themselves in, and Annie's voice, saying: "Ah! Wouldn't the boys like the fun of seeing us undress and bathing, this lovely warm day"; to which we heard Rosa laughingly reply: "I don't mind if they do see me, if I don't know it, dears. There's something delightful in the thought of the excitement it would put the dear fellows in. I know I should like Frank to take a fancy to me; I'm nearly in love with him already, and have read that the best way a girl can madly excite the man she wishes to win is to let him see all her charms, when he thinks she is unconscious of his being near."

"Well, there's no fear of our being seen here, so I am one for a good romp. Off with your clothes, quick; it will be delicious in the water," exclaimed Sophie.

The undressing was soon accomplished, excepting chemises, boots, and stockings, as they were evidently in no hurry to enter the water.

95

"Now," said Sophie, with a gay laugh, "we must make Rosa a free woman, and examine all she's got. Come on, girls, lay her down, and turn up her smock."

The beautiful girl only made a slight feint of resisting, as she playfully pulled up their chemises, exclaiming: "You shan't look at my fanny for nothing. La! Polly has got no hair on her fly trap yet. What a pretty pouting slit yours is, Annie. I think you have been using the finger of a glove made into a little cock for Sophie, and told her to bring home from school for you."

She was soon stretched on her back on the soft mossy grass, her face covered with burning blushes, as her pretty cunt was exposed to view, ornamented with its chevelure of soft red hair; her beautiful white belly and thighs shining like marble in the bright sunlight. The three sisters were blushing as well as their friend, and delighted at the sight of so much loveliness.

One after another, they kissed the vermilion lips of their friend's delightful slit, and then turning her on her face, proceeded to smack the lily white bottom of their laughing, screaming victim, with their open hands.

Smacks and laughter echoed through the grove, and we almost fancied ourselves witnesses to the games of real nymphs. At last she was allowed to rise on her knees, and then the three sisters in turn presented their cunts to their friend to kiss. Polly was the last, and Rosa, clasping her arms firmly round my youngest cousin's buttocks, exclaimed: "Ah! Ah! You have made me feel so rude, I must suck this little hairless jewel," as she glued her lips to it, and hid her face almost from sight, as if she would devour Polly's charms there and then. The young girl, flushed with excitement, placed her hands on Rosa's head, as if to keep her there, whilst both Annie and Sophie, kneeling down by the side of their friend, began to caress her cunt, bosom, and every charm they could tickle or handle.

This exciting scene lasted for five or six minutes, till at last they all sank down in a confused heap on the grass, kissing and fingering in mad excitement.

Now was our time. We had each provided ourselves with little switches of twigs, and thus armed we seemed to drop from the clouds upon the surprised girls, who screamed in fright and hid their blushing faces in their hands.

They were too astonished and alarmed to jump up, but we soon commenced to bring them to their senses, and convince them of the reality of the situation.

"What rude! what lascivious ideas! slash away Frank!" I cried, making my swish leave its marks on their bottoms at every cut.

"Who would have thought of it, Walter? We must whip such indecent ideas out of their tails!" he answered, seconding my assault with his sharp, rapid strokes.

They screamed both from pain and shame, and springing to their feet, chased round the lawn; there was no escape. We caught them by the tails of their chemises, which we lifted up to enable us to cut at their bums with more effect. At last we were getting quite out of breath, and beginning fairly to pant from exhaustion, when Annie suddenly turned upon me, saying, "Come, come, girls, let's tear their clothes off, so they shall be quite as ashamed as we are, and agree to keep our secret!" The others helped her, and we made such a feeble resistance that we were soon reduced to the same state in which we had surprised them, making them blush and look very shamefaced at the sight of our rampant engines of love.

Frank seized Miss Redquim round the waist, and led the way into the summer-house, myself and his sisters following. The gentlemen then producing the wine, &c. from the buffet, sat down with a young lady on each knee, my friend having Rosa and Polly, whilst Annie and Sophie sat with me; we plied the girls with several glasses of champagne each, which they seemed to swallow in order to drown theirsense of shame. We could feel their bodies quiver with emotion as they reclined upon our necks, their hands and ours groping under shirts and chemises in every forbidden spot; each of us had two delicate hands caressing our cocks, two delicious arms around our necks, two faces laid cheek to cheek on either side, two sets of lips to kiss, two pairs of bright and humid eyes to return our ardent glances; what wonder then that we flooded their hands with our spurting seed and felt their delicious spendings trickle over our busy fingers.

Excited by the wine, and madly lustful to enjoy the dear girls to the utmost, I stretched Sophie's legs wide apart, and sinking on my knees, gamahuched her virgin cunt, till she spent again in ecstasy, whilst dear Annie was doing the same to me, sucking the last drop of spend from my gushing prick; meanwhile Frank was following my example, Rosa surrendered to his lascivious tongue all the recesses of her virginity as she screamed with delight and pressed his head towards her mount when the frenzy of love brought her to the spending point; Polly all the while kissing her brother's belly, and frigging him to a delicious emission.

When we recovered a little from this exciting pas de trois, all bashfulness was vanished between us, we promised to renew our pleasures on the morrow, and for the present contented ourselves by bathing all together, and then returned to the house for fear the girls might be suspected of something wrong for staying out too long.

(To be continued.)

BREAK

Sporting Life, 6th August, 1879. - Mr. F. JACOBS. - We are pleased to hear that this gentleman, although severely crushed and bruised by his fall while riding Mrs. Jones at Southport in the Consolation Stakes, is going on as well as his friends could wish, and it is hoped he is quite out of danger. Query. - Was he riding a St. George, or was it a genuine toss off with its neck nearly broken? - Ed.

MISS COOTE'S CONFESSION, OR THE VOLUPTUOUS EXPERIENCES OF AN OLD MAID

In a series of Letters to a Lady Friend.

*

Letter III

My Dear Nellie,

I told you in my last how easily for me the affair of the nectarines passed over, but I was not long to go free with a whole skin. The General had evidently booked me in his mind for a good dressing the first time I should give him a pretext for punishment.

Strange to say, my first terrible punishment and dreadful cutting up of poor Jemima, related in my last letter, had very little effect, except, if possible, to render me rather more of a daredevil. I longed to pay off both Sir Eyre and Mrs. Mansell. but could think of no possible plan of effecting my revenge at all satisfactorily; if I could but do it properly, I was quite indifferent to what they might wreak upon me.

Jane could offer no suggestion, so I resolved to act entirely alone, and pretended to let it all drop, but sundry little annoyances were continually happening to different members of the family, even to myself. The General was very angry, and particularly furious, when, one day he found some of his flagellation books seriously torn and damaged, but could fix the blame on no one; indeed, I rather fancy he strongly suspected Jemima had done it out of revenge. Next Mrs.

Mansell got her feet well stung one night by nettles placed in her bed; she and Sir Eyre always were the principal sufferers, and, as a climax, two or three days afterwards, the General got his flesh considerably scratched and pricked by some pieces of bramble, cleverly hid in his bed, under the sheet, so as to be felt before they could be seen, it being his practice to throw back the upper bed clothes, and then, laying himself full length, pull them over him again. His backside first felt the pricks, which made him suddenly start from the spot, but only to get his hands, feet, legs, and all parts of his body well lacerated before he could get off the bed. I saw the sheet next day all spotted with the blood, for he was fearfully scratched, and pieces of the thorns stuck in his flesh.

Mrs. Mansell had to get out of bed in a hurry to attend the poor old fellow, and was occupied a long time in putting him to rights, returning in about an hour's time, and making haste into bed, quite unsuspicious of any lurking danger (she had already been in it) when, prick - prick - prick! "Ah! my God! The devil's been here whilst I was away," she screamed.

Jemima, Jane, and myself, ran to her room, and found her terribly scratched, especially on her knees; there were suppressed smiles on all our faces, and Jemima looked really pleased.

Mrs. Mansell.- "Ah! What a shame to serve me so. It's one of you three, and I believe it's Jemima."

Jemima.- "I couldn't help smiling, ma'am; you did scream so, and I thought you had no feeling."

Mrs. Mansell.- "You impudent hussey, Sir Eyre shall know of this."

Jemima, Jane, and myself, all declared our innocence, but in vain; there evidently would soon be a grand punishment drill for her, if not for all three.

The housekeeper and the General were both too sore for nearly a week, and, in fact, many of the thorns remained in their flesh, and one in Mrs. Mansell's knee kept her very lame, Sir Eyre had to wait ten days before he could enter into any kind of an investigation.

At last the awful day arrived; we were all mustered in the punishment room, the General seated in his chair (it was after dinner, as usual), and we were all in evening costume.

Sir Eyre.- "You all know why I have called you together. Such an outrage as Mrs. Mansell and myself suffered from cannot be passed over; in fact, if neither Miss Rosa, Jemima, nor Jane will confess the crime, I have resolved to punish all three severely, so as to be sure the real culprit gets her deserts. Now, Rosa, was it you? for if not you, it was one of the others."

Answer.- "No grandfather, besides, you know all sorts of tricks have been played upon me."

Sir Eyre.- "Well, Jemima, what do you say, yes or no?" Jemima.- "Good Lord, sir! I never touched such thorns in my life!" Sir Eyre.- "Jane, are you guilty or not, or do you know anything of it?" Jane.- "Oh! Dear! No, sir! Indeed, I don't!"

Sir Eyre.- "One of you must be a confounded story-teller. Rosa, as a young lady, I shall punish you first. Perhaps we may get a confession from one of you before we've done."

Then turning to Mrs. Mansell, "Prepare the young lady; she didn't get such a birching as she ought to have had the other day, but if it takes all night, the three of them shall be well trounced. Jane and Jemima lend a hand."

My thoughts were not so much upon what I should feel myself, as the anticipation of the fine sight the others would present, and hoping to again realize the pleasant sensations I had experienced when Jemima was so severely punished. They soon removed my blue silk dress, and fixed me to the horse, but the General interposed; he had a different idea.

"Stop! Stop!" he cried. "Let Jemima horse her." So I was released, and having my petticoats well fastened over my back, I was at once mounted on her strong stout back, my arms round her neck, being firmly held by the wrists in front, and my legs also tied together under her waist, leaving me beautifully exposed and bent so as to tighten the skin. Mrs. Mansell was about to open my drawers when Sir Eyre says: "No! No! I'm going to use this driving whip. Jemima, just trot around the room. I can reach her now."

Then giving a sharp flick with the whip, which quite convinced me of its efficacy: -

"Now, miss! What have you to say for yourself? I believe you know all about it." Slash! Slash! Slashing with the whip, as Jemima, evidently enjoying it, capered round the room; each cut made my poor bottom smart with agony.

"Oh! Oh! Ah! Grandfather!" I cried. "It's a shame to punish me, when you know I'm innocent. Oh! Ah-r-r-re," as he slashed me without mercy. I could feel I was getting wealed all over, but my drawers prevented the flesh from being cut.

Presently he ordered a halt, saying: "Now, Mrs. Mansell, let's have a look at her naughty bottom, to see if the whip has done any good."

Mrs. Mansell, carefully opening my drawers behind, exclaims, "Look, look, sir. you've touched her up nicely, what beautiful weals, and how rosy her bottom looks."

Sir Eyre.- "Aye, aye, it's a beautiful sight, but not half pretty enough yet. Mrs. Mansell, do you finish her off with the birch."

I felt assured of catching it in good earnest now. The General lit a cigar, and composed himself in his easy chair to enjoy the scene. Mrs. Mansell selected a fine birch of long, thin, green twigs, and leaving my drawers open behind, ordered Jemima to stand in front of her.

Mrs. Mansell, whisking her birch, said, "I feel sure this young lady is in the secret, but we shall get nothing out of her, she is so obstinate, but I will try my best. Sir Eyre. Now, Miss Rosa, tell the truth if you want to save your bottom; are you quite as sure as ever of your own innocence?" whisking and slashing me smartly and with great deliberation, making the blows fall with a whacking sound, not inconsiderably adding to the previous warmth of my posteriors, which smart and tingle terrifically at each cut.

"Oh! ah! how unjust," I screamed, to relieve myself as much as possible. "Oh, ah! If I do know I can't tell, it's a secret. Oh! have mercy!" thus trying to serve a double purpose to be let off lightly myself, by making them think someone else did it, and so transfer their fury to Jane and Jemima, whose whipping I hoped to enjoy.

Mrs. Mansell.- "Ha! ha! 'tis wonderful how the birch has improved you, my dear Miss Rosa, you're not nearly so obstinate as you were, but if you won't tell, you must be punished as an accessory. I'm sorry to do it, but it doesn't hurt you quite so awfully, does it?" thrashing away without a moment's respite; my poor bottom is beginning to be finely pickled, and I can feel the blood trickling down my legs inside my drawers.

"Hold! Hold!" cries the General, excitedly; "it's that devil

Jemima; you've punished Rosa enough, try Jane next, if she knows anything we'll make her confess, and then the impudent red-headed Jemima shall catch it finely. We're getting at the truth, Mrs. Mansell."

I am let down, and the General orders Jane to take my place on the stout back; I let my clothes down with a thrill of excitement, and thanking Sir Eyre for his kindness, make myself busy in helping to arrange poor Jane's posteriors for slaughter, and pin up her skirts to her shoulders, exposing her fine, plump bottom, and beautiful thighs and legs, the latter encased in pink silk stockings, set off by red satin slippers and blue garters with silver buckles.

Sir Eyre.- "How now, Jane, you hussey, do you dare to come into my presence without drawers, how indecent, it's like telling me to 'ax my arse,' you impudent girl; how do you like that;" giving her a tremendous under cut so that the birch fairly well wealed the flesh right up to her mossy crack; "it's all very well, in the heat of a birching, but to expose your nakedness like that so impudently is quite another," continuing to cut away in apparently great indignation.

Jane.- "Ah! Ah! Ah-a-r-re! My God, sir, have pity, Mrs. Mansell didn't allow us time to dress, and in the hurry I couldn't find my drawers to put on, and she was angrily calling me to come, and not keep her waiting. So I thought duty must be considered before decency. Oh! Oh! Oh! sir, you are cruel. Oh! have mercy, I'm as innocent as a babe!" as she is in terrible agony from the under cuts, which have already drawn the blood; she writhes and struggles so, Jemima can hardly stand under her plunging figure.

Sir Eyre.- "Well, well, I'm inclined to forgive you about the drawers, as I always like everybody to consider duty before everything, but how about putting the thorns in the bed; you must know about that, and it's your duty to confess."

Jane.- "Oh! Oh! Ah-r-r-re, I can't tell, I'm innocent, how can I split upon another? Oh, you'll kill me, sir! I shall be confined to my bed for weeks if you cut me up so!"

Sir Eyre.- "Fiddlesticks, bottoms get well quicker than that, Jane, don't be alarmed, but I shall punish you a good deal more if you don't confess it was Jemima did it. Now wasn't it Jemima? Wasn't it Jemima! wasn't it Jemima!" thundering at her both with voice and rod and drawing the blood finely.

104

The victim is almost ready to faint, still I could see the usual indications of voluptuous excitement, notwithstanding the agony she must be in, but at last she seems quite exhausted, and ceasing to writhe and wriggle as if she no longer felt the cruel blows whilst her shrieks sink to a sobbing. "Yes, yes! oh! yes."

Sir Eyre.- "Ha! Ha! Ha!" laughing in anticipation of getting the real culprit. "Yes! yes! she's confessed at last, let her down now, poor thing," throwing away the stump of the worn-out rod; "she took a lot before she would give way, but It's bound to come out."

Poor Jane is let down in a pitiable condition, and Jemima hisses something about "lying chit" between her teeth, as I assist Mrs. Mansell to tie her to the horse, and having pinned up her skirts, I opened her drawers so as fully to expose the snow white beauties of her fine rump.

Sir Eyre.- "Open them as wide as possible, Rosa; the mean creature, to let others suffer for her own crime, and even take delight in helping to punish them."

Jemima.- "It's all a lie, Sir Eyre, I never had anything to do with it, and they have turned round on me so they may enjoy the sight of my flogging. Oh! oh! this is a cruel house, pay me my wages and let me go."

Sir Eyre, chuckling.- "You'll get your wages, or at least your deserts, you sneaking wretch."

Jemima (is crimson with shame and fury), exclaiming- "I'm not so much a sneak as somebody else who's done it; I'll die before I own what I never did."

Sir Eyre.- "Don't let us waste any more time on the obstinate hussey. Let's try what a good birch will do," slashing her two or three times severely on her bottom, and bringing out the rosy flush all over the surface of its firm broad cheeks.

"See how her bottom blushes for her," laughed the General, "but it will soon have to weep blood," increasing the force of his blows, and drawing weals at every stroke.

Jemima.- "Oh! Oh! Sir Eyre! how can you believe a lying girl like Jane, won't I box her ears for her when I get over this, the spiteful thing, to say it's me!"

Sir Eyre.- "You're the spiteful one. Will you box her ears? Do you really mean that, you strong, impudent donkey! I shall soon have to try something better than a birch on you, it's not severe enough; you shall beg Jane's pardon before I've done with you; you may be strong and tough, but we'll master that somehow; how do you like it? I hope you don't feel it, Jemima; I don't think you do, or you would be more penitent," said he, in a fury. "I wish I had a good bramble here to tear your bottom with, perhaps you might feel that."

Jemima.- "Oh! No! Pray don't. I didn't do it, and wouldn't have done such a thing to my worst enemy. Oh! Oh! Sir! Have mercy, I'm being murdered. You'll bleed me to death," as she feels the blood trickling down her thighs.

Sir Eyre.- "You're too bad to be easily killed. Why don't you confess, you wicked creature?" Then turning to Mrs. Mansell: "Don't you think, ma'am, she's got too many things on? I am not given to cruelty, but this is a case requiring greater severity than usual."

Mrs. Mansell.- "Shall we reduce her to her chemise and drawers, so you can administer the extreme penalty?"

Sir Eyre.- "Yes! Yes! It will give a little time to recover my breath. She's taken all the strength out of me."

We now strip all her petticoats off, and undo her stays, fully displaying the large fine plump globes of her splendid bosom, with their pretty pink nipples; then she is fastened up again, and stands with her wrists fastened well above her head. She has her fawn-coloured kid gloves, and the net, as usual, up to her elbows, so as to set off her arms and hands to the best advantage. She has nothing but chemise and drawers to hide her fine figure; but before commencing again, the General orders the latter to be entirely removed and her chemise to be pinned up to the shoulders; then turning to me, he said:

"Rosa, my dear, it's all through that wicked young woman you have been punished. I don't wish to teach anyone to revenge themselves, but as Mrs. Mansell is hardly well enough, and I am in want of a little more rest, I think you could take this whip," handing me a fine ladies' switch, with a little piece of knotted cord at the end. "There, you know how to use it; don't spare any part of her bottom or thighs."

This was just what I had been longing for, but did not like to volunteer. With a glance of triumph towards poor Jane (who was gradually getting over her own punishment, and beginning to take interest in what was going forward), I took the whip, and placed myself in position to commence. What a beautiful sight my victim presented, her splendid plump back, loins, and buttocks fully exposed to view, whilst the red wealed flesh of her bottom, smeared with blood, contrasted so nicely with her snow-white belly in front, ornamented on the Mons Veneris with a profusion of soft curly hair of a light sandy colour; and her legs being fixed widely apart, I could see her pink bottom-hole; and the pouting lips of her cunny just underneath; further down stretched the splendid expanse of her well-developed thighs, as white as her belly; then she was also dressed in crimson silk stockings, pretty garters and fawn-coloured slippers to match her gloves. My blood seemed to boil at the sight of so much loveliness, which I longed to cut into ribbons of wealed flesh and blood.

Sir Eyre.- "Go on, Rosie, what makes you so slow to begin? You can't do too much to such an obstinate thing; try and make her beg Jane's pardon."

Rosa.- "She looks very nice, but I'm afraid the whip will cut her up so, grandfather. Now, Jemima, I'm going to begin, does that hurt you?" giving her a light cut on her tender thighs, where the tip of the whip left a very plain red mark.

Jemima.- "Oh! Oh! Miss Rosa, be merciful; I've never been unkind to you; how nicely I rode you on my back when you were punished."

Rosa.- "Yes! and enjoyed the fun all the time, you cruel thing; you knew what I was getting, but I could tell you were delighted to horse me," giving three or four smart cuts across her loins, and registering every blow with a fine angry-looking weal. "There! There! There! Ask my pardon, and Jane's pardon for your threats. Will you box her ears, will you!" cutting sharply at every question in some unexpected part; no two strokes follow each other in the same place.

Victim.- "A-r-r-re, have mercy. I was sorry for you, Miss Rosie. Oh! You're as hard as Sir Eyre. You'll cut me to pieces with that whip," she sobs out, her face crimson with the conflicting emotions of fear, rage, and obstinacy.

Rosa.- "Now, Jemima, your only chance is to beg our pardon, and confess your crime; you know you did it, you know you did it, you obstinate wench," cutting the flesh in every direction, and making the blood flow freely all down the thighs on to her stockings.

The victim writhes and shrieks with pain at every blow, but refuses to admit her fault, or beg pardon. The sight of her sufferings seemed to nerve my arm, and add to my excitement, the blood seemed delicious in my eyes, and I gradually worked myself up, so that I felt such gushing thrilling sensations as to quite overcome me. The whip was dropped in exhaustion, and I sank back on a seat in a kind of lethargic stupor, yet quite conscious of all that was going on.

Sir Eyre.- "Why, Rosie, I thought you were stronger than that. Poor thing, your punishment was too much for you. I'll finish the culprit. If she won't confess, she must be executed, that's all," snatching up another whip, much heavier than the one I had used, and with three tips of cord on the end. "You won't confess, won't you, you obstinate wicked creature? My blood boils when I think how I punished the other two innocent girls," he exclaimed, cutting her fearfully on the calves of her legs, knocking the delicate silk of the stockings to pieces, and wealing and bruising her legs all over. The victim cannot plunge about, as her ankles are fastened, but she moans with agony, and shrieks and sobs hysterically in turns at this terrible attack. The General seems beside himself with rage, for he next turns to her beautiful white shoulders, and slashes them about, fearfully cutting through the skin and deluging poor Jemima with her own blood.

Sir Eyre.- "I shall murder her; I can't help it; she's made me quite mad." His cuts wind round her ribs, and even weal the beauties of her splendid bosom, and stains the snowy belly with their blood.

Jemima (in low broken sobs).- "Oh! Oh! Mercy! Let me die! Don't torture an innocent thing like me any longer." She seems going to faint, when Mrs. Mansell interposes, saying: "It is enough; more may do serious injury."

Sir Eyre (gasping for breath).- "Oh! Oh! I know you are right to take me away, or I shall really murder her."

The bleeding victim is a pitiable and terrible sight as we release her from the ladder; she is scarcely able to stand; her boots covered with blood, and little pools of the sanguineous fluid stand on the floor; and we had to administer a cordial before she was able to be supported to her room, where she was confined to her bed for several days.

I had now had all the revenge I was so anxious to inflict; but the great avenger of all, to my great grief, soon removed poor old grandfather from this world, and left me indeed an orphan. Being still very young, my guardians under Sir Eyre's will placed me at Miss Flaybum's Academy to finish my education, and the old home was broken up, and inmates scattered.

I shall send you some of my school experiences in my next, and remain, Dear Nellie,

Yours affectionately. Rosa Belinda Coote.

(To be continued.)

CURIOUSITY

"Pray, mama," said Sally, "what's the meaning of Hush?"

"My dear," said mama, "what makes you ask such a question?"

"Because I asked Fanny what made her belly stick out so, and she answered, 'Hush.'

CHARLIE COLLINGWOOD'S FLOGGING,

by

Etoniensis.

Eighteen years of age, with round limbs, and broad shoulders, tall, rosy and fair,

And all over his forehead and temples, a forest of curly red hair;

Good in the playing fields, good on the water, or in it, this lad:

But at sums, or at themes, or at verses, oh! ain't Charlie Collingwood bad?

Six days out of seven, or five at the least, he's sent up to be stripped;

But it's nuts for the lower boys always, to see Charlie Collingwood whipped;

For the marks of the birch on his bottom are more than the leaves on a tree,

And a bum that has worn so much birch out, as Charlie's, is jolly to see.

When his shirt is turned up, and his breeches, unbuttoned, hang down to his heels,

From the small of his back, to the thick of his thighs is one mass of red weals.

Ted Beauchamp last year began keeping a list of his floggings and he

Says, they come; in a year-and-a-half, to a hundred and sixty and three.

And you see how this morning, in front of the flogging block silent he stands,

And hitches his waistband up slightly, and feels his backside with his hands.

Then he lifts his blue eyes to the face of the Master, nor shrinks at his frown,

Nor at sight of the birch, nor at sound of the sentence of judgment, "Go down."

Not a word, Charlie Collingwood says, not a syllable, piteous or pert;

But goes down with his breeches unbuttoned, and Errington takes up his shirt.

And again we can see his great naked red bottom, round, fleshy, and plump.

And the bystanders look from the Master's red rod, to the schoolboy's red rump:

There are weals over weals, there are stripes upon stripes, there are cuts after cuts,

All across Charlie Collingwood's bottom, and isn't the sight of it nuts?

There, that cut on the fleshiest part of the buttocks, high up on the right,

He got that before supper last evening, oh! isn't his bottom a sight?

And that scar that's just healed, don't you see where the birch cut the flesh?

That's a token of Charlie's last flogging, the rod will soon stamp it afresh.

And this morning you saw he could hardly sit down, or be quiet in Church;

It's a pleasure to see Charlie's bottom, it looks just cut out for the birch.

Now, look out, Master Charlie, it's coming: you won't get off this time, by God!

For your Master's in, oh, such a wax! and he's picked you out, oh, such a rod!

Such a jolly good rod, with the buds on, so stout, and so supple and lithe,

You've been flogged till you're hardened to flogging, but won't the first cut make you writhe?

You've been birched till you say you don't care as you used for a birching! Indeed?

Wait a bit, Master Charlie, I'll bet the third cut or the fourth makes you bleed.

Though they say a boy's bottom grows harder with whipping, and times make it tough.

Yet the sturdiest boy's bottom will wince if the Schoolmaster whips it enough.

Aye, the stoutest posteriors will redden, and flinch from the cuts as they come.

If they're flogged half as hard as the Master will flog Charlie Collingwood's bum.

We shall see a real jolly good swishing, as good as a fellow could wish;

Here's a stunning good rod, and a jolly big bottom just under it - Swish!

Oh, by Jove, he's drawn blood at the very first cut! in two places by God!

Aye, and Charlie's red bottom grows redder all over with marks of the rod.

And the pain of the cut makes his burning posteriors quiver and heave.

And he's hiding his face-yes, by Jove, and he's wiping his eyes on his sleeve!

Now; give it him well, Sir, lay into him well, till the pain makes him roar!

Flog him, then, till he stops, and then flog him again, till he bellows once more!

Ah, Charlie, my boy, you don't mind it, eh do you? it's nothing to bear.

Though a small boy may cry for a flogging, that's natural, but Charlie don't care.

That's right, Sir, don't spare him! that cut was a stinger, but Charlie don't mind;

All the rods in the kingdom would only be wasted on Charlie's behind,

At each cut, how the red flesh rises, the red weals tingle and swell!

How he blushes! I told you the Master would flog Charlie Collingwoodwell.

There are long red ridges and furrows, across his great, broad, nether cheeks,

And on both his plump, rosy, round buttocks, the blood stands in drops and in streaks.

Well hit, Sir! Well caught! how he drew in his bottom, and flinched from the cut!

At each touch of the birch on his bum, how the smart makes it open and shut!

Well struck, Sir, again, how it made the blood spin! there's a drop on the floor,

Each long, fleshy furrow grows ruddy, and Charlie can bear it no more.

Blood runs from each weal on his bottom, and all Charlie's bottom is wealed

'Twill be many a day ere the scars of this flogging are thoroughly healed.

Now just under the hollow of Charlie's bare back, where the flanks are aslope.

The rod catches and stings him, and now at the point where the downward ways ope;

Round his flanks, now like serpents, the birchen twigs twining bend round as they bite,

And you see on his naked, white belly, red ridges, where all was so white.

Where between his white thighs, something hairy, the body's division reveals.

Falls the next cut, and now Charlie Collingwood's bottom is all over weals.

Not a twig on the rod, but has raised a red ridge on his flesh, not a bud,

But has drawn from his naked and writhing posteriors, a fresh drop of blood.

And the Schoolmaster warms to his work now, as harder and harder he hits,
And picks out the most sensitive places, as though he'd cut Charlie to bits.
"So you'll fidget and whisper in school-time, and make a disturbance in Church?
"Can't sit still, Master Charlie, eh, can't you? Well, what do you think of the birch?
"Oh, it hurts you so, does it, my boy, to sit down, since I flogged you last night?
"It was that made you fidget all church time? Indeed, you can't help it, please God-
"By the help of the birch, Master Charlie, I'll teach you to help it, please God-
"If you don't mend your manners in future, it shan't be for want of a rod.
"You're a big boy, no doubt, to be flogged; the more shame for you, Sir, at your age-
"But as long as you're here, I shall flog you," he lays on the cuts in a rage.
"Aye, and if you were older and bigger, you'd come to the flogging block still—
"Boys are never too big to be beaten!" he lays on the birch with a will,
"if a boy's not too old to go wrong, Sir, he can't be too old to be whipped;
"So take that!" and he lays on the rod, till the twigs all with crimson are tipped.

There are drops of the boy's blood visible now, on each tender young bud-
Blood has dropped on his trousers, and Charlie's bare bottom is covered with blood.
But I'd rather be shut up for days, in a hole you would scarce put a dog in.
And brought out once a day to be birched, than have missed

Charlie Collingwood's flogging.

How each cut brings the blood to his forehead, and makes him bite half through his lips!

How the birch cuts his bottom right over, and makes the blood spin from his hips!

How his brawny bare haunches, all bloody, and wealed, with red furrows like ruts,

Shrink quivering with pain at each stroke, that revives all the smart of past cuts!

How the Schoolmaster seems to hit harder, the birch to sting more at each blow!

Till at last Charlie Collingwood, writhing with agony, bellows out,"Oh!"

That was all; not a word of petition; a single short cry and no more;

And the younger boys laugh, that the birch should have made such a big fellow roar.

For a moment, the Master too pauses; but not for a truce or a parley:

Then the birch falls afresh, on the bloody wealed flesh, with "Take that, Master Charlie."

All the small boys are breathless and hushed; but they hear not a syllable come,

They hear only the swish of the birch, as it meets Charlie Collingwood's bum.

And the Master's face flushes with anger; he signs to Fred Fane with a nod;

And Freddy reluctantly hands him another stout, supple birch rod.

And again as he flogs Charlie Collingwood's bottom, his face seems aflame;

At each cut he reminds him of this thing or that, and rebukes him by name.

Each cut makes the boy's haunches quiver, and scores them all over afresh;

You can trace where each separate birch twig has marked Charlie Collingwood's flesh.

Till the Master, tired out with hard work, and quite satiate with flogging for once.

With one last cut, that stings to the quick, bids him rise for an Obstinate Dunce.

From the block Charlie Collingwood rises, red faced, and with tumbled red hair.

And with crimson hued bottom, and tearful blue eyes, and a look of "Don't Care."

Then he draws up his breeches, and walks out of school with a crowd of boys dogging

The heels of their hero, all proud to have seen Charlie Collingwood's flogging.

FINIS.

INTERMISSO

"Jack, my boy, what a devil of an appetite you have this morning," said one friend to another as they were breakfasting at their hotel. "And so would you," replied Jack, "if you had only had a whore's tongue and a toothbrush in your mouth since yesterday!"

Madame Rollin had three monkeys, of which one was a she; and the lady used to amuse herself with watching their tricks. "It is curious," said she, "to observe them, for while one of them is caressing the other, the third comforts himself!"

Her expression was "suffices for himself"!!

Meaning Masturbation of Course!!!

LADY POKINGHAM; OR THEY ALL DO IT

Giving an Account of her Luxurious Adventures,

*

Part III

(Continued.)

Christmas came, and with it arrived several visitors, all young ladies and gentlemen of about our own ages, to spend the festive season with us; our entire party consisted of five gentlemen and seven ladies, leaving out the aunt, who was too old to enter into youthful fun and contented herself with being a faithful housekeeper, and keeping good house, so that after supper every evening we could do almost as we liked; myself and Alice soon converted our five young lady friends into tribades like ourselves, ready for anything, whilst Frederick prepared his young male friends. New Year's Day was his eighteenth birthday, and we determined to hold a regular orgy that night in our corridor, with Lucy's help. Plenty of refreshments were laid in stock, ices, sandwiches, and champagne; the aunt strictly ordered us all to retire at one A.M. at latest, so we kept her commands, after spending a delicious evening in dancing and games, which only served to flush us with excitement for what all instinctively felt would be a most voluptuous entertainment upstairs.

The aunt was a heavy sleeper, and rather deaf, besides which Frederick, under the excuse of making them drink his health, plied the servants first with beer, then with wine, and afterwards with just a glass of brandy for a nightcap; so that we were assured they would also be sound enough, in fact two or three never got to bed at all.

Frederick was master of the ceremonies, with Alice as a most useful assistant. As I said before, all were flushed with excitement and ready for anything; they were all of the most aristocratic families, and our blue blood seemed fairly to course through our veins. When all had assembled in Alice's apartment they found her attired in a simple, long chemise de nuit. "Ladies and gentlemen," she said, "I believe we are all agreed for an out and out romp; you see my costume, how do you like it?" and a most wicked smile, "I hope it does not display the contour of my figure too much," drawing it tightly about her so as to show the outline of her beautiful buttocks, and also displaying a pair of ravishing legs in pink silk stockings.

"Bravo! Bravo! Bravo Alice! we will follow your example," burst from all sides. Each one skipped back to his or her room and reappeared in mufti; but the tails of the young gentlemen's shirts caused a deal of laughter, by being too short.

Alice.- "Well, I'm sure, gentlemen, I did not think your undergarments were so indecently short."

Frederick, with a laugh, caught hold of his sister's chemise, and tore a great piece off all around, so that she was in quite a short smock, which only half-covered her fair bottom.

Alice was crimson with blushes, and half inclined to be angry, but recovering herself, she laughed, "Ah! Fred, what a shame to serve me so, but I don't mind if you make us all alike."

The girls screamed, and the gentlemen made a rush; it was a most exciting scene; the young ladies retaliated by tearing the shirts of their tormentors, and this first skirmish only ended when the whole company were reduced to a complete state of nudity; all were in blushes as they gazed upon the variety of male and female charms exposed to view.

Frederick, advancing with a bumper of champagne.- "We've all heard of Nuda Veritas, now let's drink to her health; the first time we are in her company, I'm sure she will be most charming and agreeable."

All joined in this toast, the wine inflamed our desires, there was not a male organ present but what was in a glorious state of erection.

Alice.- "Look, ladies, what a lot of impudent fellows, they need not think we are going to surrender anyhow to their youthful lust; they shall be all blindfolded, and then we will arm ourselves with good birch rods, then let it be everyone for themselves and Cupid's dart for us all."

"Hear, hear," responded on all sides, and handkerchiefs were soon tied over their eyes, and seven good birch rods handed round to the ladies. "Now, gentlemen, catch who you can," laughed Alice, slashing right and left into the manly group, her example being followed by the other girls; the room was quite large enough and a fine romp ensued, the girls were as lithe and active as young fawns, and for a long time sorely tried the patience of their male friends, who tumbled about in all directions, only to get an extra dose of birch on their plump posteriors before they could regain their feet.

At last the Honble. Miss Vavasour stumbled over a prostrate gentleman, who happened to be the young Marquis of Bucktown, who grasped her firmly round the waist, and clung to his prize, as a shower of cuts greeted the writhing pair.

"Hold, hold," cried Alice, "she's fairly caught and must submit to be offered as a victim on the Altar of Love."

Lucy quickly wheeled a small soft couch into the centre of the room. The gentlemen pulled off their bandages, and all laughingly assisted to place the pair in position; the lady underneath with a pillow under her buttocks, and the young marquis, on his knees, fairly planted between her thighs. Both were novices, but a more beautiful couple it would be impossible to conceive; he was a fine young fellow of eighteen, with dark hair and eyes, whilst her brunette style of complexion was almost a counterpart of his; their eyes were similar also, and his instrument, as well as her cunny, were finely ornamented with soft curly black hair; with the skin drawn back, the firey purple head of his cock looked like a large ruby, as, by Frederick's suggestion, he presented it to her luscious-looking vermilion gap, the lips of which were just slightly open as she lay with her legs apart. The touch seemed to electrify her, the blushing face turned to a still deeper crimson as the dart of love slowly entered the outwarks of her virginity. Fred continued to act as mentor, by whispering in the young gallant's ear, who also was covered with blushes, but feeling his steed fairly in contact with the throbbing matrix of the lovely girl beneath him, he at once plunged forward to the attack, pushing, shoving, and clasping her round the body with all his strength, whilst he tried to stifle her cries of pain by glueing his lips to hers. It was a case of Veni, Vidi, Vici. His onset was too impetuous to be withstood, and she lay in such a passive favourable position that the network of her hymen was broken at the first charge, and he was soon in full possession up to the roots of his hair. He rested a moment, she opened her eyes, and with a faint smile said, "Ah! It was indeed sharp, but I can already begin to feel the pleasures of love. Go on now, dear boy, our example will soon fire the others to imitate us," heaving up her bottom as a challenge, and pressing him fondly to her bosom. They ran a delightful course, which filled us all with voluptuous excitement, and as they died away in a mutual spend, someone put out the lights. All was laughing confusion, gentlemen trying to catch a prize, kissing and sighing.

I felt myself seized by a strong arm, a hand groped for my cunny, whilst a whisper in my ear said: "How delightful! It's you, dear little Beatrice. I can't make a mistake, as yours is the only hairless thing in the company. Kiss me, dear, I'm bursting to be into your tight little affair." Lips met lips in a luscious kiss. We found ourselves close to Alice's bed, my companion put me back on it, and taking my legs under his arms, was soon pushing his way up my longing cunny. I nipped him as tightly as possible; he was in ecstasies and spent almost directly, but keeping his place, he put me, by his vigorous action, into a perfect frenzy of love. Spend seemed to follow spend, till we had each of us done it six times, and the last time I so forgot myself as to fairly bite his shoulder in delight. At length he withdrew, without telling his name. The room was still in darkness, and love engagements were going on all round. I had two more partners after that, but only one go with each. I shall never forget that night as long as a breath remains in my body.

Next day I found out, through Fred, that Charlie Vavasour had been my first partner, and that he himself believed he had had his sister in the melee, which she afterwards admitted to me was a fact, although she thought he did not know it, and the temptation to enjoy her brother was too much for her.

This orgie has been the means of establishing a kind of secret society amongst the circle of our friends. Anyone who gives a

122

pressure of the hand and asks: "Do you remember Fred's birthday?" is free to indulge in love with those who understand it and I have since been present at many repetitions of that birthday fun.

We returned to school, and I kept up a regular correspondence with Frederick, the letters to and fro being enclosed in those of Alice. Time crept on, but as you can imagine as well or better than I can relate all the kinds of salacious amusements we girls used to indulge in, I shall skip over the next few years till I arrived at the age of eighteen; my guardians were in a hurry to present me at Court, and have me brought out[1] in hopes that I might soon marry and relieve them of their trust.

Alice was so attached to me that since my first visit to her home, she had solicited her aunt to arrange with my guardians for my permanent residence with her during my minority, which quite fell in with their views, as it enabled me to see more society, and often meet gentlemen who might perhaps fall in love with my pretty face.

Lady St. Jerome undertook to present both Alice and myself; she was an aunt, and mentioned in her letter that unfortunately a star of the first magnitude would also be presented at the same drawing room, but still we might have a faint chance of picking up young Lothair, the great matrimonial prize of the season, if he did not immediately fall in love with the beautiful Lady Corisande, and that we should meet them both at Crecy House, at the Duchess's ball, in celebration of the presentation of her favourite daughter, for which she had obtained invitations for us. For nearly three weeks we were in a flutter of excitement, making the necessary preparations for our debut. My mother's jewels were reset to suit the fashion of the day, and every three or four days we went to town to see our Court milliner.

In company with Alice and her aunt, we arrived at Lord St. Jerome's town residence in St. James' Square, the evening before the eventful day; her ladyship was a most charming person of about thirty, without family, who introduced us before dinner to her niece, Miss Clare Arundel, Father Coleman, the family confessor, and Monsignore Berwick, the chamberlain of Pio Nono. The dinner was exquisite, and we passed a delightful evening, amused by the quiet humour of the confessor, and the sparkling wit of Monsignore, who seemed to studiously avoid religious subjects. Miss Arundel, with her beautiful, pensive, violet eyes, and dark brown golden hair, seemed particularly fascinated by the sallies of the latter, whilst there was a something remarked by both Alice and myself, which led us to suspect the existence of some curious tie between the two ecclesiastics and the ladies of the household.

Lord St. Jerome was not in town. At our special request, Alice and myself shared the same room, which opened into a spacious corridor, at one end of which was a small chapel or oratory. Our minds were so unsettled by the thoughts of the morrow, and also hopes of meeting some of our old friends in town, especially the Vavasours, that sleep was quite banished from our eyes; suddenly Alice started up in bed, with, "Hist! there's someone moving about the corridor." She sprang out of bed and softly opened our door, whilst I followed and stood close behind her. "They're gone into the oratory," she said. "I saw a figure just in the act of passing in; I will know what is going on; we can easily slip into some of the empty rooms, if we hear anyone coming."

So saying, she put on her slippers and threw a shawl over her shoulders, and I followed her example; ready for any kind of adventure, we cautiously advanced along the corridor, soon we arrived at the door of the oratory, and could hear several low voices inside, but were afraid to push the door ajar for fear of being observed.

"Hush!" whispered Alice, "I was here when quite a little girl, and now remember that old Lady St. Jerome, who has been dead some time, used to use this room next to the chapel, and had a private entrance made for herself direct from the room into the oratory. If we can get in there," she said, turning the handle, "we shall be in a fine place to see everything, as the room is never used, and said to be haunted by the old lady." The door yielded to her pressure, and we slipped into a gloomy room, just able to see a little by the light of the moon.

(To be continued.)

A TASTE FOR FOREIGNERS

(Imitated from Martial.)

To the French, to the Germans and Swedes,

Easy Harriet, you give up your charms;
Italians and Russians besides
Have all had their turns in your arms;
You despise not the Dutch, nor the Danes,
Mulattoes, or Negroes, or Finns;
In you they may all quench their flames.
Whatever the tint of their skins.
You reject the capless concerns,
Or the circumcised Turk or the Jew;
In short, every nation by turns.
Has had an erection in you;
Your fancy is truly uncommon,
The reason I wish I could find;
While by birth you're a true Englishwoman,
That no true English prick's to your mind.

ADULTERY'S THE GO!

(Song before the time of the New Divorce Court.)

When we were boys the world was good,
But that is long ago;
Now all the wisest folks are lewd
For Adultery's the go.
The go, the go, the go,

Adultery's the go!

Quite tired of leading virtuous lives,
Though spotless as the snow.
Among the chaste and pious wives,

Adultery's the go.

The go, the go, the go, &c.
Long life then to the House of Lords.
They know a thing or two;
You see from all their grand awards,

That Adultery's the go.

The go, the go, the go, &c.
And Lady Barlow, Mrs. Hare.
Case, Clarke, and Bolders;
Teed, Ashton, James, and all declare

Adultery's the go.

The go, the go, the go, &c.
Some husbands still are jealous,
And guard the furbelow,
But spite such prudish fellows.

Adultery's the go.

The go, the go, the go, &c.
Horn'd cuckolds were mad raging bulls,
A century ago;
Now, they're tame oxen, silly fools,

For Adultery's the go.

The go, the go, the go, &c.
Then, hey for Doctors' Commons,
With horned beasts arow;
For man's delight, and woman's,

Adultery's the go.

HER VERY SOUL

On Sundays, in a church like this,
I joy to face the blushing Miss,
Eye within eye, agog for bliss,
Through touching not, I only kiss,
Her very soul! Her very soul!
She falls at once into my plan,
I guess she prays, behind her fan,h
"Oh, for a man! A real man!
To satiate, as he only can,
Her very soul! Her very soul!
Heavens! what a glance! see her suck,
And lick her lips, on fire for cock.
I see her frisky bottom buck,
While with the prick of lust I fuck,
Her very soul! Her very soul!

128

FIRST RONDEAU

Ten years ago, on Christmas day,
Fair Helen stole my heart away,
I went to church - but not to pray.
Ten years ago.
To pray? Yes - pray to Helen's eyes;
Ah! would that we had been more wise;
To-day, she would not recognize
Him whom she kissed in ecstasies,
Ten years ago.

SECOND RONDEAU.

Again we've met, and now I find,
Her still more luscious to my mind;
She was not to such pranks inclined.
Ten years ago.
Though now a second time she's wed.
Hers is a most lascivious bed;
Though thirty years she now has sped.
She fucks still better than she did.
Ten years ago.

LINES WRITTEN UNDER HER PORTRAIT

Such Helen was! religious, young and fair;
A faithful spouse, and blest with babies dear;
But in the church, while week by week she prayed,
An amorous noble long her charms surveyed;
Sunday by Sunday, seated near her pew.

He kept the goddess of his heart in view;
And when the Tenth Command was duly read,
"I covet thee," his burning glances said-
Her humble rank forbade acquaintance free,
Yet high enough it was to guard her modesty;
Her husband was a gamester fierce and rude,
He fled the town, and other loves pursu'd;

She on her jointure fair remained at home,
Close guarded by his mother and her own;
Two months at church, she stood the siege of sighs,
Silence, that spoke, and eloquence of eyes;
Could virtue longer last? at length she fell;
No more, no more, can happy lovers tell.

And mark the sequel! rashly she had sworn
She ne'er would to her faithless lord return;
Her prudent lover urged a course more wise,
His vigour had more force than his advice;

She would not listen, till her swelling zone,
Proved his kind counsel wiser than her own.

Just at that juncture her good man returned,
In time to adopt the babe, that proves him horn'd;
The wedding ring upon her hand you see
Is not her wedding ring, 'twas given by me;
The one her husband gave her, here, here, behold!

Around my finger wreaths its hallow'd gold;
Her diamond brooch and clasps all brightly shine,
His gifts indeed! the locks they hold are mine;
Far, far away, I now her absence mourn,
Grant me, O Venus! grant a quick return;
Keep Helen virtuous, till again we meet,
And revel in the bliss so naughty and so sweet.

UP THE CHIMNEY

When Captain Jones of Halifax,
Was put in winter quarters,
His landlady, a widow, had
The prettiest of daughters.

The Captain sued her lovingly,
The girl was gay and ready
To join her lot with his and be
The noble Captain's lady.

Their wedding was deferred; but soon.
Impatient for the pleasure,
He found his way into her room,
And swiv'd her at his leisure.

The chambermaid, who set to rights
The different pots and pans.
Warn'd mistress there was ne'er a drop
In that of this young man's.

The mother asked him tenderly,
"As you're to wed my daughter.
Pray tell me why - my dear young man,
Why - why - you make no water?"

"Ah, Madam!" cried he, "cannot you
The real reason guess?
The fact is that I go to bed,
So full of tenderness.

I get eager for the bliss,
I feel so stiff and hot,
That really I'm obliged to piss
Right up the Chimney Pot."

INTERLUDE

In the wars in India, in the year 1800, Major Torrens's party was pursuing some of the enemy. One day, while they were dining and very merry, a sergeant came and reported to the Major that two prisoners were brought in, one old and one young. The Sergeant requested orders regarding them. The Major merrily answered: "Oh, take them away and frig them." The Sergeant retired. In an hour he returned, and respectfully made this report: "Please your honour, we have frigged the young one. but we can't make the old man's cock stand."

This story was related to me, in 1818, by Torrens, who was then an old General at Madras.

NURSERY RHYMES.

There was a young lady of Harrow.
Who complained that her Cunt was too narrow,
For times without number
She would use a cucumber,
But could not accomplish a marrow.

There was a young lady of Glasgow,
And fondly her lover did ask, "Oh,
Pray allow me a fuck,"
But she said, "No, my duck,
But you may, if you please, up my arse go."

There was a young man had the art
Of making a capital tart,
With a handful of shit,
Some snot and a spit,
And he'd flavor the whole with a fart.

There was an old man of Connaught.
Whose prick was remarkably short,
When he got into bed
The old woman said,
"This isn't a prick, it's a wart."

There was a gay Countess of Bray,

And you may think it odd when I say,
That in spite of high station,
Rank and education,
She always spelt Cunt with a K.

There was an old parson of Lundy,
Fell asleep in his vestry on Sunday;
He awoke with a scream,
"What, another wet dream,
This comes of not frigging since Monday."

There was a strong man of Drumrig,
Who one day did seven times frig;
He buggered three Sailors,
Four Jews and two Tailors,
And ended by fucking a pig.

There was an Old Man of the Mountain.
Who frigged himself into a fountain,
Fifteen times had he spent.
Still he wasn't content.
He simply got tired of the counting.

There was a young man of Nantucket.
Who went down a well in a bucket;
The last words he spoke.
Before the rope broke,
Were, "Arsehole, you bugger, and suck it."

A native of Havre de Grace
Once tired of Cunt, said "I'll try arse."
He unfolded his plan
To another young man,
Who said, "Most decidedly, my arse!"

NOTE

At the Parish Church, South Hackney, by the Rev. C. A. White, John Henry Bottomfeldt, of Hamburgh, to Sarah Jane Greens, of South Hackney. (Vide "Daily Telegraph," January 3, 1875).

How lovely everything now seems
When joined in one by Hymen's belt,
For now John Henry has his Greens,
And Sarah Jane her Bottom-feldt.

VOLUME IV

* * * * *

Published Monthly

Oct. 1879

SUB-UMBRA, OR SPORT AMONG THE SHE-NOODLES

(continued)

After luncheon Frank smoked his cigarette in my room; the events of the morning had left both of us in a most unsettled and excited state. "I say, old fellow," he exclaimed, "by Jove! it's quite impossible for me to wait till to-morrow for the chance of enjoying that delicious Rosa; besides, when there are so many of us together there is just the chance of being disappointed; no, no, it must be this very night if I die for it; her room is only the other side of my sisters'."

I tried to persuade him from doing anything rashly, as we could not yet be certain that even excited and ready as she had shown herself, that she was prepared to surrender her virginity so quickly. However, arguments and reasonings were in vain. "See," he exclaimed, "the very thoughts of her make my prick ready to burst," opening his trousers and letting out his beautiful red-headed cock, as it stood in all its manly glory, stiff and hard as marble, with the hot blood looking ready to burst from his distended veins; the sight was too exciting for me to restrain myself, the cigarette dropped from my lips, and going upon my knees in front of him, I kissed, sucked, frigged, and played with his delicious prick till he spent in my mouth with an exclamation of rapture, as I eagerly swallowed every drop of his copious emission. When we had a little recovered our serenity, we discussed the best plans for the night, as I was determined to have my share of the amusement, which Frank most willingly agreed to, provided he was to go first to Rosa's room, and prevail upon her to consent to his ardent suit; then when all seemed to be en regie, I was to surprise them in the midst of their fun, and join in the erotic frolic.

After dinner we adjourned to the drawing-room, where a most pleasant evening was enlivened by music and singing, leaving Frank turning over the leaves for Rosa and Polly, as they sang "What Are the Wild Waves Saying." Annie and Sophie whispered to me that they should like a short stroll in the garden by moonlight, so opening the window, a few steps brought us on to the soft gravel path, where we could walk with an almost noiseless tread. Papa and Mama were in the library playing cribbage, and we felt sure that Frank and Rosa would not run after us, so passing rapidly down a shady walk, with one arm round each of the dear girl's waists, and alternately kissing one and the other of them, we soon arrived at a very convenient spot, and the instinct of love allowed me to guide the willing girls into a rather dark arbour without the least demur on their part.

"How lovely the honeysuckle smells!" sighed Sophie, as I drew them both down by my side in the corner, and began a most delicious kissing and groping in the dim obscurity.

"Not so sweet as your dear little pussey," said I, playfully twisting my fingers in the soft down around the tight little grotto of love which I had taken possession of.

"Oh! Oh! Mind, Walter dear!" she sighed softly, as she clung round my neck.

"Will you let me kiss it as I did Annie's this morning, my little pet, it will give you such pleasure; there's nothing to be bashful or shamefaced about here in the dark; ask your sister if it wasn't delicious."

ANNIE. - "Oh! let him, Sophie dear, you will experience the most heavenly sensations."

Thus urged she allowed me to raise her clothes, and recline her backwards in the corner, but this would not admit of Annie having

140

her fair share of the game, but as she was now all aflame with excited expectation, there was no difficulty in persuading her to kneel over my face as I reclined on my back at full length on the seat; lovely hands at once let my eager prick out of his confined position in my trousers, and as I commenced to suck and gamahuche Sophie, I felt that the dear Annie had taken possession of my cock for her own special benefit.

"Oh! let me kiss you, Sophie dear, put your tongue in my mouth," said Annie, straddling over me, and putting away my excited engine of love up her own longing crack, and beginning a delightful St. George; I clasped the younger girl firmly round the buttocks with one arm. Whilst with my right hand I found and rubbed her stiff little clitoris to increase the excitement from the lascivious motions of my tongue in her virgin cunny.

Annie was in a frenzy of voluptuous enjoyment, she bounced up and down on my prick, and now and then rested for a moment to indulge in the exquisite pleasure of the devil's bite, which she seemed to possess to a most precocious extent, the folds of her cunt contracting and throbbing upon my swelling prick in the most delicious manner.

Sophie was all of a tremble, she wriggled herself most excitedly over my mouth, and I licked up her virgin spendings as they came down in a thick creamy emission.

"Oh! Oh! Oh!" she sighed, hugging and kissing Annie in fondest abandon. "What is it, dear? I shall choke, Walter. There's something running from me; it's so delicious. Oh! What shall I do?"

Annie and myself met at this moment in a joint spend, which left us in an ecstatic lethargy of love, and the two sisters almost fainted upon my prostrate body.

When we had recovered a little, I sat up between the loving sisters.

Sophie, throwing her arms round my neck, quite smothered me with her burning kisses, as she whispered in my ear: "It was indeed pleasure, dear Walter. Is that one of the delights of love, and what was Annie doing, for she was as excited as I was?"

"Can't you guess, darling?" I replied, taking her hand and placing it upon my still rampant cock. "That is what she played with."

"But how?" whispered the innocent girl. "She was kissing and sucking my tongue deliciously all the while, but seemed as if she could not keep still a moment."

"She had that plaything of mine up her cunny, my dear, and was riding up and down upon it till we all fainted with the pleasure at the same time. You shall have a real lesson in love next time, and Annie won't be jealous, will you, dearest?"

ANNIE. - "No, no, we must all be free to enjoy all the games of love without jealousy. I wonder how Frank is getting on with Rosa by this time. We must now make haste back to the house."

Sophie was anxious for more explanations as to the arts of love, but was put off till another time; and all being now in a cooler state of mind, we returned to the house, where we found Frank repeating the game of the morning, by gamahuching Rosa, whilst Polly was gone out of the room.

The red-haired beauty was covered with blushes, as she suddenly dropped her clothes on our entrance, and only recovered from her crimson shamefacedness when Annie laughingly assured her that we had been enjoying ourselves in the same manner.

"Oh! How rude and indecent of us all," exclaimed Rosa, "but who can resist the burning touches of a handsome young fellow like your brother; he was so impudent, and it sends such a thrill of voluptuousness through the whole frame," commencing to sing, "It's naughty, but it's nice."

The supper bell rang, and, after a light repast, we all separated to our rooms. Frank came into my chamber to join in a cigarette and glass of grog before finally retiring.

"It's all right for to-night, old fellow," he exclaimed, as soon as we were seated for our smoke. "I begged Rosa to let me kiss all her charms, in her own room without the inconvenience of clothes. She made some objections at first, but finally consented not to lock the door, if I promised not to go beyond kissing, on my honour as a gentleman."

He was too impatient to stop long, and, after only one smoke, cut off to his room. Undressing myself as quickly as possible, I went to him, and escorted him to the door of his lady-love; it was unlocked, and he glided noiselessly into the darkened chamber. She was evidently awake and expecting his visit, for I could hear their rapturous kissing and his exclamation of delight as he ran his hands over her beautiful figure. "My love, I must light the candles to feast my eyes upon your extraordinary beauties. Why did you put out the lights?" She made some faint remonstrances, but the room was soon a blaze of light from half-a-dozen candles.

I was looking through the keyhole, and eagerly listening to every word.

"My love, let us lay side by side and enjoy feeling our bodies in naked contact before we begin the kissing each other's charms."

I could see that his shirt and her chemise de nuit were both turned up as high as possible, and his prick was throbbing against her belly. He made her grasp it in her hand, and pulling one of her legs over his thighs, was trying to place the head of his eager cock to the mark between her legs.

"Ah! No! No! Never! You promised on your honour, sir!" she almost screamed in alarm, and struggling to disengage herself from his strong embrace. "No! No! Oh! No! I won't, indeed!"

His previous soft manner seemed in a moment to have changed to a mad fury, as he suddenly rolled her over on her back, keeping his own legs well between her thighs.

"Honour! Honour!" he laughed. "How can I have honour when you tempt me so, Rosa? You have driven me mad by the liberties I have been allowed. Resistance is useless. I would rather die than not have you now, you dear girl."

She struggled in desperate silence for a few moments, but her strength was unequal to his; he gradually got into position, and then taking advantage of her exhaustion, rapidly and ruthlessly completed her ravishment.

She seemed insensible at first, and I took advantage of her short unconsciousness to steal into the room, and kneel at the foot of the bed, where I had a fine view of his blood-stained weapon, thrusting in and out of her shattered virginity. After a little she seemed to begin to enjoy his movements, especially after the first lubricating injection of his love juice. Her buttocks heaved up to meet his thrusts, and her arms clung convulsively round his body, and seemed reluctant to let him withdraw, until both seemed to come together in a luscious spend.

As they lay exhausted after this bout, I advanced and kissed the dear girl, and as she opened her eyes, I placed my hand across her mouth to stop any inconvenient scream of surprise, and congratulated her on having so nicely got rid of her troublesome virginity, and claimed my share of the fun, drawing her attention to the rampant condition of my cock in contrast to Frank's limp affair. I could see she was now eager for a repetition of the pleasure she had only just begun to taste. Her eyes were full of languishing desire as I placed her hand upon my prick.

In accordance with our previously devised arrangements she was persuaded to ride a St. George upon me, my cock was inserted in her still tender cunt, with great care, and allowed slowly to get his position, but the excitement was too great for me, with an exclamation of delight I shot a stream of sperm up into her very entrails, this set her off, she began slowly to move upon me, her cunt gripping and throbbing upon the shaft most deliciously, and we were soon running another delightful course; this was too much for Frank, his cock was again as hard as iron, and eager to get in somewhere, so kneeling up behind her he tried to insert his prick in her cunt alongside of mine, but found it too difficult to achieve, then the charming wrinkled orifice of her pink bottom-hole caught his attention, the tip of his affair was wet with our spendings, and his vigorous shoves soon gained an entrance, as I was holding her fast and she was too excited to resist anything, only giving a slight scream as she found him slip inside of the part she thought was only made for another purpose. I asked them to rest a few moments and enjoy the sensation of feeling where we were, our pricks throbbing against each other in a most delicious manner, with only the thin membrane of the anal canal between them; it made us spend immediately to the great delight of Rosa, who at once urged us to go on.

This was the most delightful bout of fucking I had ever had; she made us do it over and over again and, when we were exhausted, sucked our pricks up to renewed cockstands. This lasted till the dawn of day warned us of the necessity of precaution, and we retired to our respective rooms.

(To be continued.)

144

MISS COOTE'S CONFESSION, OR THE VOLUPTUOUS EXPERIENCES OF AN OLD MAID

In a series of Letters to a Lady Friend.

*

Letter IV

My Dear Nellie,

I promised in my last to relate a few of my school experiences, so now I will try and redeem the promise.

Her house was situated at Edmonton, so famous for Johnny Gilpin's ride. It was a large spacious mansion, formerly belonging to some nobleman, and stood in its own grounds. What were called the private gardens, next the house, were all enclosed in high walls, to prevent the possibility of any elopements.

Beyond these, in a ring fence, there were several paddocks for grazing purposes, in which Miss Flaybum kept her cows and turned the carriage horses, when not in use (which was all the week), for we only took coach, carriage, or whatever the conveyance might be, on Sundays, when we were twice regularly driven to the village church, nearly one-and-a-half miles distant, for Miss Flaybum's ladies could not be permitted, upon even the finest days, to walk there. We always called the vehicles coaches, although they were a kind of nondescript vehicle, and having nearly three dozen young ladies in the establishment, we filled three of them, and formed quite a grand procession as we drove up to the church door, and there was generally quite a little crowd to see us alight or take our departure, and, as the eldest girls assured us, it was only to see if we showed our legs, or displayed rather more ankle than usual. We were very particular as to silk stockings, and the finest and most fashionable boots we could get to set off our limbs to greatest advantage, and, in wet weather, when we were obliged to hold up our dresses rather more, I often observed quite a titter of admiration amongst the spectators, who curiously, as it seemed to us, were mostly the eldest gentlemen of the place, who evidently were as anxious to keep their sons away from the sight of our blandishments as Miss Flaybum could possibly wish; at any rate, it seemed to be understood to be highly improper for any young gentleman ever to present himself at what we called our Sunday levee.

We were never allowed to walk in the country roads, but on half-holidays or any special occasions, in fine weather, our governess would escort us into paddocks, and a little wood of three or four acres, which was included within the ring fence, where we indulged in a variety of games free from observation.

The school was very select, none but the daughters of the aristocracy or officers of the army or navy being admitted to the establishment; even the professions were barred by Miss Flaybum, who was a middle-aged maiden lady, and a very strict martinet.

Before I went to this school, I always thought such places were conducted with the greatest possible propriety as to morals, etc., but soon found that it was only an outward show of decorum, whereas the private arrangements admitted of a variety of very questionable doings, not at all conducive to the future morality of the pupils, and if other fashionable schools are all conducted upon the same principles, it easily accounts for that aristocratic indifference to virtue so prevalent in my early days.

The very first night I was in the house (we slept, half-a-dozen of us, in a fine large room), I had not been settled in bed with my partner more than an hour before quite a dozen girls invaded the room, and pulled me out of bed, to be made free of the establishment, as they call it.

They laid me across one of the beds, stuffed a handkerchief in my mouth to prevent my cries, and every one of them slapped my naked bottom three times and some of them did it very spitefully, so that my

146

poor rump tingled and smarted as if I had had a good birching.

Laura Sandon, my bedfellow, who was a very nice kind-hearted girl comforted and assured me all the girls had to go through the same ordeal as soon as they came to the school. I asked her if the birch was ever used in the establishment.

"Bless you, yes," she replied; "you are a dear love of a girl, and I shall be sorry to see you catch it," kissing me and rubbing my smarting bottom. "How hot it is, let's throw off the bedclothes and cool it," she added.

"Let's look at her poor bottom," said Miss Louise Van Tromp, a fine fair Dutch girl; "shall we have a game of slaps before Mdlle. Fosse (the French Governess) comes to bed?"

"Yes, come, Rosa dear, you'll like that, it will make you forget your own smarts; get up Cecile and Clara for a romp," addressing the Hon. Miss Cecile Deben and Lady Clara Wavering, who with the French Governess made up the six occupants of our room. "You know Mdlle. won't say anything if she does catch us."

We were soon out of bed, with our nightdresses thrown off, and all quite naked: Laura, a thin, fair girl with soft large blue eyes, always such a sure indication of an amorous disposition; Cecile, a nice plump little dear with chestnut hair and blue eyes. Lady Clara, who was just upon eighteen, was dark, rather above the middle height, well-proportioned, with languid, pensive hazel eyes, whilst Louise Van Tromp was a fat Dutch girl, with grey eyes and splendidly developed figure.

It was a beautiful sight, for they were all pretty, and none of them showed any shamefacedness over it, evidently being quite used to the game; they all gathered round me, and patted and kissed my bottom, Cecile saying, "Rosie, I'm so glad you've no hair on your pussey yet, you will keep me in countenance; these other girls think so much of their hairiness, as if they were old women; what's the use of it Laura, now you have got it," playing with the soft fair down of Miss Sandon's pussey.

LAURA. - "You silly thing, don't tickle so, you'll be proud enough when you get it."

LADY CLARA. - "Cecile, dear, you've only to rub your belly on mine a little more than you do, that's how Laura got hers."

LOUISE. - "Rosie, you shall rub your belly on mine; Clara is too

147

fond of Cecile. I can make yours grow for you, my dear," kissing me and feeling my mount in a very loving way.

LAURA. - "Listen to Grey Eyes Greedy Guts, you'd think none of us ever played with the Van Tromp. Rosie, you belong to me."

We now commenced the game of slaps, which in reality was similar to a common children's sport called "touch." Ours was a very large room, the three beds, dressing tables, washstands, &c, all arranged round the sides, leaving a good clear space in the centre.

LADY CLARA. - "I'll be 'Slappee' to begin," taking her station in the middle of the room.

Each girl now placed herself with one hand touching a bedstead or some article of furniture, and as Clara turned her back to any of us we would slip slyly up behind and give a fine spanking slap on her bottom, making it assume a rosy flush all over; but if she could succeed in returning the slap to anyone before they regained their touch, the one that was caught had to take her place as "Slappee."

We all joined heartily in the game, keeping up a constant sound of slaps, advancing and retreating, or slipping up now and then to vary the amusement, in which case the unfortunate one got a general slapping from all the players before she could recover herself, making great fun and laughter. You would think such games would soon be checked by the governess, but the rule was never to interfere with any games amongst the pupils in their bedrooms. Just as our sport was at its height the door opened, and Mdlle. Fosse entered, exclaiming, "Ma foi, you rude girls, all out of bed slapping one another, and the lamp never put out, how indelicate, young ladies, to expose yourselves so; but Mdlle. Flaybum does not like to check you out of school, so it's no business of mine, but you want slapping, do you? How would you like to be cut with this, Mdlle. Coote?" showing me a very pretty little birch rod of long thin twigs, tied up with blue velvet and ribbons. "It would tickle very differently to hand slapping."

"Ah! Mademoiselle, I've felt much worse than that three times the size and weight. My poor old grandfather, the General, was a dreadful flogger," I replied.

MADEMOISELLE. - "I thought girls were only whipped at school. You must tell me all about it, Miss ROSA."

"With great pleasure. I don't suppose any of you have seen such punishment inflicted as I could tell you of," I replied.

The young French lady had been rapidly undressing herself as this conversation was going on. She was very dark, black hair over a rather low forehead, with a most pleasing expression of face, and fine sparkling eyes, hid under what struck me as uncommonly bushy eyebrows. She unlaced her corset, fully exposing a beautiful snowy bosom, ornamented with a pair of lovely round globes, with dark nipples, and her skin, although so white, had a remarkable contrast to our fairer flesh. There seemed to be a tinge of black somewhere, whereas our white complexion must have been from an original pink source, infinitely diluted.

MADEMOISELLE. - "Ah! You Van Tromp, ou est ma robe de chambre? Have you hidden it?"

LOUISE. - "Oh! Pray strip and have a game with us. You shan't have the nightdress yet."

MADEMOISELLE. - "You shall catch it if you make me play; your bottom shall smart for it."

We all gathered round her, and although she playfully resisted, she was soon denuded of every rag of clothing. We pulled off her boots and stockings; but what a beautiful sight she was, apparently about twenty-six, with nicely rounded limbs, but such a glorious profusion of hair, that from her head, now let loose, hung down her back in a dense mass, and quite covered her bottom, so that she might have sat on the end of it, whereas her belly, it is almost impossible to describe it, except by calling it a veritable "Foret Noire." The glossy black curling hair, extending all over her mount, up to her navel, and hanging several inches down between her thighs.

"There, Mdlle. Rosa," she exclaimed sitting on the edge of her bed, "did you ever see anyone so hairy as I am? It's a sign of a loving nature, my dear," nipping my bottom and kissing me as she hugged my naked figure to hers. "How I love to caress the little featherless birdies like you. You shall sleep with me sometimes. The Van Tromp will be glad to change me for Laura."

"We cannot allow that," cried two or three of the others together. "Now you shall be 'Slappee' with your birch, Mdlle."

"Very well," said the lively French lady. "You'll get well touched up if I do catch any of you."

Then we commenced our game again, and she switched us finely, leaving long red marks on our bottoms when she succeeded in making a hit. Her own bottom must have smarted from our smacks, but she seemed quite excited and delighted with the amusement, till at last she said: "Oh! I must be birched myself, who will be the schoolmistress?"

LAURA. - "Oh! Let Rosa! She will lecture you as if you were a culprit, and give us an idea of good earnest punishment. Will you, Rosa? it will amuse us all. Just try if you can't make Mademoiselle ask your pardon for taking liberties with you, do, there's a dear girl."

"Yes! Yes! That will be fine," cried the others, especially Lady Clara, who was already seated on her bed with Cecile as her partner.

LOUISE. - "Mdlle. wants Rosa for her bedfellow to-night, so let her tickle her up with the birch; don't spare her, Rosie, she's so hard to hurt; come Laura, let us enjoy the night together."

Thus urged I took up the rod and, flourishing it lightly in the air, said, laughing. "I know how to use it properly, especially on naughty bottoms, which have the impudence to challenge me; now, Mdlle., present your bottom on the edge of the bed, with your legs well apart, just touching the floor, but I must have two of them to hold you down; come, Laura and Louise, each of you hold one arm, and keep her body well down on the bed. There, that will do just so, hold her securely, don't let her get up till I've fairly done."

ROSA. - "Mdlle. Fosse, you are a very wicked young lady to behave so rudely to me as you have done; will you beg my pardon, and promise never to do so any more; do you feel that and that?" giving a couple of stinging little switches across her loins.

MADEMOISELLE. - "Oh! no! I won't apologize, I do love little featherless chits like you!"

ROSA. - "You call me a chit, do you? I'll teach you a little more respect for your schoolmistress; is that too hard, or perhaps you like that better," giving a couple of slashing cuts on her rounded buttocks, which leave long red marks, and make her wriggle with pain.

MADEMOISELLE. - "Ah! Ah! Ah-r-r-re, that's too hard. Oh! Oh! You do cut, you little devil," as I go on sharper and sharper at every stroke, making her writhe and wriggle under the tingling switches which mark her bottom in every direction.

ROSA. - "Little devil, indeed, you shall beg my pardon for that too, you insulting young lady, how dare you express yourself so to your governess, your bottom must be cut to pieces, if I can't subdue such a proud spirit. There -there - there!" cutting away, each stroke going in on the tender parts of her inner thighs. "Will you be rude again? Will you insult me again, eh? I hope I don't hurt you too much, pray tell me if I do. Ha! Ha!! Ha!!! you don't seem quite to approve of it by the motions of your impudent bottom," cutting away all the while I was speaking, each stroke with deliberation on some unexpected place, till her bum was rosy all over, and marked with a profusion of deep red weals.

Mademoiselle makes desperate efforts to release herself, but Lady Clara and Cecile also help to keep her down, all apparently highly excited by the sight of her excoriated blushing bottom, adding their remarks, such as, "Bravo, Bravo, Rosie. you didn't think she would catch it so, how delightful to see her writhe and plunge in pain, to hear her scream, and help to keep her down," till at last the surprised victim begs and prays for pardon, crying to be let off, with tears in her eyes.

This is the end of the night's amusements, for all now resume their night chemises and retire, Mdlle. taking me to sleep with her. "Ah! Ma cherie" she exclaimed, as the lamp was put out and I found myself in her arms, "how cruelly you have warmed my poor bottom, and have you really seen worse than that, Rosie?"

"Oh! far, far worse, Mdlle., I've seen the blood flow freely from cut up bottoms," I replied, at the same time repaying her caresses and running my hand through the thick curly, hair of her mount, as she was feeling and tickling my pussey. "There, there," she whispered; "nip me, squeeze that little bit of flesh," as my hand wandered to the lips of her hairy retreat, "tickle me as I do you," putting me in great confusion by her touches, for I had never experienced anything like it before, except the melting, burning sensations of the same parts at the conclusion of my previous flagellations.

This dalliance continued between us for some months, and I soon became an apt pupil in her sensual amusements, being emboldened by her freedoms, and heated by a most curious desire to explore with my fingers everything about that hairy paradise. Meanwhile she tickled and rubbed the entrance of my slit in a most exciting manner, and suddenly she clasped me close to her naked body (our chemises were turned up so we might feel each other's naked flesh), and kissed my lips in such a rapturous, luscious manner as to send a thrill of ecstasy through my whole quivering frame, her fingers worked nervously in my crack, and I felt quite a sudden gush of something from me, wetting her fingers and all my secret parts, whilst she pressed me more and more, wriggling and sighing, "Oh! oh! Rosa, go on, rub, rub"; then suddenly she stiffened herself out straight and seemed almost rigid as I felt my hand deluged with a profusion of warm, thick, sticky stuff.

After a few moments' rest she recovered herself, and said to me: "Listen! listen! The others are all doing the same. Can't you hear their sighs? Oh! Isn't it nice, Rosa dear?"

"Yes! Yes!" I whispered, in a shamefaced manner, for I seemed to know we had indulged in some very improper proceeding. "Oh! Mademoiselle, do they all do it? It's so nice of you to play with me so."

MADEMOISELLE. - "Of course they do. It's the only pleasure we can have in school. Ah! You should be with Lady Clara or the Van Tromp, how they spend and go on in their ecstasy."

"What is spending?" I whispered. "Is that the wet I felt on my fingers when you stiffened yourself out?"

MADEMOISELLE. - "Yes, and you spent too, little bashful. Didn't the birching make you feel funny?"

ROSA (in a whisper). - "Even when I have been cut so that the blood flowed down my legs, at last I suddenly got dulled to the pain, and came an over with a delicious hot burning melting feeling which drowned every other sensation."

MADEMOISELLE. - "Rosa, you're a little darling. Would you like to feel it over again? I know another way, if you only do to me exactly as I do to you, will you?"

I willingly assented to the lovely Francaise, who, reversing our positions, laid on her back, and made me lay my body on hers, head downwards. Our chemises were turned up close under our arms, so as fully to enjoy the contact of our naked bodies, and I found my face buried in the beautiful mossy forest on her mount, and felt Mademoiselle, with her face between my thighs, tickling my little slit with something soft and warm, which I soon found out was her tongue. She passed it lovingly along the crack and inside as far as it would reach, whilst one of her fingers invaded my bottom-hole, and worked in and out in a most exciting way.

Not to be behind hand, I imitated all her movements, and burying my face between her thighs, revelled with my tongue and fingers in every secret place. She wriggled and tossed her bottom up and down, especially after I had succeeded in forcing a finger well up the little hole and worked it about, as she was doing to me. Although it was all so new to me, there was something so exciting and luscious in it all; to handle, feel, and revel in such a luxuriously covered pussey and bottom excited me more and more every moment; then the fiery touches of her tongue on my own burning orifices so worked me up that I spent all-over her mouth, pressing my slit down upon her in the most lascivious manner, just as her own affair rewarded me in the same manner. After a little time we composed ourselves to sleep, and with many loving expressions and promises of future enjoyment.

This was my experience the first night of my school life, and I need not weary you with repetitions of the same kind of scene, but simply tell you that it was enacted almost every night, and that we constantly changed our partners, so that was the cause of my acquiring such a penchant for female bedfellows, especially when they have been previously well warmed by a little preparatory flagellation.

Miss Flaybum was a stern disciplinarian in her school, and we often came under her hands, when she wielded the birch with great effect, generally having the culprit horsed on the back of a strong maid servant, who evidently delighted in her occupation.

I must be drawing this letter to a close, but will give you one illustration of how we were punished in my time.

I cannot exactly remember what my offense was, but it was probably for being impertinent to Miss Herbert, the English governess, a strict maiden lady of thirty, who never overlooked the slightest mark of disrespect to herself.

Miss Flaybum would seat herself in state upon a kind of raised dais, where she usually sat when she was in the school-room. Miss Herbert would introduce the culprit to her thus:

MISS HERBERT. - "Madame, this is Miss Coote, she has been disrespectful to me, and said I was an old frump."

MISS FLAYBURN. - "That is a most improper word to be used by young ladies, you have only to take away the f, and what remains, but a word I would never pronounce with my lips, it's too vulgar. Miss Rosa Belinda Coote (she always addressed culprits by their full name), I shall chastise you with the rod; call Maria to prepare her for punishment."

The stout and strong Maria immediately appears and conducts me into a kind of small vestry sacred to the goddess of flagellation, if there is such a deity; there she strips off all my clothes, except chemise and drawers, and makes me put on a kind of penitential dress, consisting of a white mobcap and a long white garment, something like a nightdress; it fitted close up round the throat with a little plain frill round the neck and down the front, being fastened by a band round the waist,

Maria now ushers me again into the presence of Miss Flaybum, all blushing as I am at the degrading costume, and ridiculous figure I must look to my schoolfellows, who are all in a titter.

Maria lays a fine bunch of fresh birch twigs (especially tied up with ribbons) at my feet, I have to pick it up and kiss it in a most respectful manner, and ask my schoolmistress to chastise me properly with it. All this was frightfully humiliating, especially the first time, for however free we might have been with one another in our bedrooms there was such a sense of mortifying shame, sure to be felt all through the proceedings.

Miss Flaybum, rising with great dignity from her seat, motions with her hand, and Miss Herbert assisted by the German governess, Frau Bildaur, at once mounted me on Maria's broad back, and pinned up the dress above my waist, then the English governess with evident pleasure opened my drawers behind so as to expose my bare bottom, whilst the soft-hearted young German showed her sympathy by eyes brimming with tears.

MISS FLAYBURN. - "I shall administer a dozen sharp cuts, and then insist upon your begging Miss Herbert's pardon," commencing to count the strokes one by one, as she whisks steadily, but with great force, every blow falling with a loud "whack," and making my bottom smart and tingle with pain, and giving assurance of a plentiful crop of weals. My red blushing bottom must have been a most edifying sight to the pupils, and a regular caution to timid offenders, two or three more of whom might expect their turn in a day or two; although I screamed and cried out in apparent anguish it was nothing to what I had suffered at the hands of Sir Eyre or Mrs. Mansell; the worst part of the punishment was in the degrading ceremony and charity girl costume the victim had to assume.

The dozen duly inflicted, I had first to beg Miss Herbert's pardon, and then having again kissed the rod, and thanked Miss Flaybum for what she called her loving correction, I was allowed to retire and resume my own apparel. I could tell you about many punishment scenes, but in my next shall have the grand finale to my school life, and how we paid off Miss Flaybum and the English governess before leaving.

And remain, dear Nellie,

Your ever loving

ROSA BELINDA COOTE.

(To be continued.)

YOUNG BEGINNERS

"Now, dear Nelly, as we are both snug in bed, give me the account you promised of all that passed at your uncle's during your visit."

Well, don't frig me so hard, or you'll cut short my story. My uncle, you know, is a widower. He has three children, Gussy, Johnny, and Janey. I was only just eighteen. So we were all well suited together, and soon became great friends. The two boys had lately come home for their holidays, and were up to every kind of fun. Our favourite place for play was the hay loft; and our chief amusement rolling down the hay one after the other. On one occasion my frock flew up in the descent, so that when I reached the bottom, my legs were all uncovered, and the little slit between them (just newly fringed with hair) was fully exposed to view.

"Oh, look!" cried Johnny, pointing to it, and throwing himself upon me. "See what she has there."

"For shame," I said, struggling to get up.

"Hold her down," cried Gussy spreading my thighs, and opening my cunt with his fingers.

"What a funny little place, Nelly. Let us have a good look. Why need you mind? You may see mine if you like. Let's all look at one another, and see which has the nicest."

"Oh, do!" cried John and Janey, "it will be great fun."

So the two boys pulled out their little pricks, and Janey, holding up her dress and pulling aside her drawers, showed us her small unfledged cunt.

"Yours is far the nicest," said Gussy to me. "For yours has hair;

we have none yet, but we shall bye-and-bye."

"How do you know?" asked Janey.

"Because I have often seen men bathing, and they all had hair about their pricks, as they call them."

"But what of women; you've never seen them bathing?"

"No, but I have seen nurse's, and she has plenty. One night, about a year ago, she was giving me a warm bath, and when she was drying me, she began tickling my little cockey; I was ashamed, but she said it was nothing to mind, that I would soon be proud enough of it, and that then I would be wanting to stick it into the chink that women have at the bottom of their belly. I coaxed her to let me feel hers. She did, and let me see it too."

"What was it like, Gussy?"

"Just like a great mouth with a beard all around it. I could nearly put my hand up into it, it was so big."

It was quite funny to see how the boys' pricks stiffened up as they felt and examined my cunt. Janey too looked on eagerly and frigged her own little slit with the handle of a battledore.

"But," said Johnny, "you have no place for getting into you here, like nurse."

"Yes, she has. See! I can push my finger up."

"Stop, Gussy, you are hurting me."

"Well, let me put my prick in. That won't hurt, I am sure."

"Do let him," cried John and Janey. "It will be such fun."

"You may try if you like," I said.

He then knelt between my open thighs, and pushed his prick about the lips of my cunt.

"Oh, he can't get it in," said Janey, "what a pity."

I began to grow excited, so I put down my hand and held his prick at the right entrance, while with my other hand on his bottom I helped to push him in.

"Oh, now it's going in, every bit of it; does it hurt you Nelly, does it hurt?"

"No dear, it feels very nice; that's the way."

Gussy, impelled by nature, shoved eagerly in and out, John and Jane laughed, but Gussy began to breathe hard, his face flushed, his eyes sparkled. "Oh!" he cried "what's going to happen, hold me Nelly," and he fell forward on my breast, as he poured forth for the first time his maiden treasure.

After that we never lost an opportunity of playing with each other's privates. Janey and I used to frig and suck the boys' pricks, and they tickled and kissed our cunts; but Gussy and I always ended with a fuck, for he had a wonderful tool for so young a lad, and enjoyed the sweet exercise thoroughly.

He told me that he had seen his father fucking a girl in the hayfield, after the labourers had gone home. She had come back to look for something. Uncle met her, drew her behind one of the stacks, tossed up her clothes, and made her lie on her back with her legs up. He then unbuttoned his trousers, took out his prick, and kneeling between her thighs, shoved it into her cunt.

"It was at the other side of the hedge, and I heard him saying, 'Come here. Maggy, I want to give you something.'

'Thanks, sir, you are very good. But I want a kiss in return.'

He kissed her loudly. Then she said: 'Oh, but, dear sir, you need not push your knee between my thighs. Ah! stop, you'll make me fall.'

"'Be quiet, Maggy, and I'll give you something more when I have done.'

"I had been searching for an opening in the hedge, and at length between the bushes I caught sight of them just as he had got her on her back, with her belly and legs all exposed. When I first saw his big red-headed prick standing out stiffly from the hair at its base, I did feel ashamed to look, but I was so eager to see Maggy's cunt, and to observe how a real fuck was performed, that I would not for the world have turned away my eyes."

"He soon got his prick in, and drove it up her cunt. She seemed used to the sport, and as he went on fucking she heaved up and down, crying, 'Give it me, dear sir, give it me, hard and strong, oh! oh!'

"'That's right, Maggy, give tongue, lift your arse, and tickle my balls.'

Maggy called out prick, cunt, arse, at every push, and their bellies smacked together, until giving one tremendous lunge, Father darted his prick into her cunt pressed her in his arms, and kissed her in great delight."

"Then he gave her something, and when she had arranged her dress, she stole quietly away."

"You should not be talking of these things, Gussy."

"No more I do, only to you, and you know I tell you everything."

About this time a new governess arrived. She was a pretty flaxen-haired girl named Lizzy. I soon remarked that Uncle was very attentive to her, and was always bringing her flowers and small presents.

She slept in a room next mine, and separated from it by a wooden partition, the two having formed but one apartment. I could hear every stir she made. I knew when she got out of bed, when she took her bath, and even when she sat on the chamber pot. I observed one day that in one spot the paper over the boards had cracked, and that there was a small open slit between them. On putting my eye close I could see into Lizzy's room quite plainly. A few nights after, when I was in bed, I heard whispering in her room. I got up softly and went to the slit. By the light of her fire, I saw Uncle with his arm round Lizzy, and heard her saying:

"Mr. C, do go away. Oh, my! Where are you dragging me? I won't sit on the bed with you. What do you mean by pushing me back. Don't attempt to raise my clothes. Oh! Where are you putting your hand? Take it away, you are very nasty. Don't lift my legs. I won't let you. You'll ruin me. You are hurting my hands."

"Well, take your hands out of the way. Here; put them on my prick if you like. Open. Open more. I tell you to keep quiet, or you'll waken Nelly."

"I won't let you put it in. You must not do it."

"Do let me, love - only just a moment. There, let it in. What's the use of all this struggling?"

"You'll kiss me. I'm so tired. What is it you want?"

"Only to fuck you my darling. To put my prick in here - into your sweet cunt and fuck you. There! There! It's getting in. Don't you feel it going up-up! How hot your cunt is. Isn't it nice?"

"Yes, that's very nice. I like that. You may fuck me now. Push it in well. Oh. yes; push. Oh!"

"Push what in, my love?"

"Your prick! Your prick; dear Mr. C."

"Where do you like me to push my prick?"

"Into my cunt! Into my cunt!"

"What is my prick doing in your cunt, Lizzy?"

"Fucking me! Fucking me! Oh! so nicely. You may fuck me as hard as you like. Oh! Oh!"

Uncle had placed her on her back with her bottom projecting over the edge of the bed, her clothes were all up, her thighs stretched wide open, and her legs resting on his shoulders. He had let down his trousers, and tucked up his shirt, so I could see his great muscular rump working vigorously back and forward, driving his stiff moist prick in and out between the hairy lips of her cunt.

I felt greatly excited, and my cunt seemed burning with heat. I could not help putting my hand on it, and squeezing the lips as hard as I could.

Just then I felt someone's arm stealing round me, and a hand placed on my mouth to stifle my cry.

Gussy whispered in my ear: "It's me. Don't say a word. Feel my prick, how stiff it is. I'll put it into your cunt this way, and fuck you from behind, but keep watching, and tell me all they are doing. What do you see?"

"I see your father fucking Lizzy. She is on her back with her bottom over the edge of the bed, her legs up on his shoulders. I can see her cunt."

"What is it like?"

"A large hairy mouth sucking his prick."

"Is he fucking still? Go on, dear Nelly; it's just coming."

"He is heaving backward and forward, faster and faster. Now he is stooping over her, clutching her in his arms. How he drives his prick into her cunt! How she bounds to meet it. There! He is done! Push, Gussy! Hold me, or I shall fall! Oh! what a nice fuck! You have a darling prick, Gussy. Now let us rest, and I'll suck it for you to make it strong again."

After a while we heard them whispering again.

"Now," said Gussy, "let us change places. Sit here with your back to the partition, and you can play with my prick, while I look through and tell you all they are doing."

I took the head of his soft little tool in my mouth, and played with his balls and bottom while he looked through the opening.

"He is kneeling down and kissing and sucking her cunt; there, he has opened wide the lips, and is looking into its deep red chink; now he is licking round it with his tongue, while he rubs his nose against

160

the hair-listen."

"What a delicious cunt you have, Lizzy; it smells so sweet, and has such thick round full lips, and although so large, the entrance itself is as tight as possible, and holds my prick like a glove. Now lie along the edge, put your hand on this poor fellow, and pet him a little before we try another bout."

"Now he is standing up, and she has her arm round his hip so as to reach his balls from behind, with her other hand she holds his prick; she is drawing up and down the soft skin, now she places its rosy head to her lips.

"Take it in your mouth, my love."

"I declare she has taken nearly half of it in; what a mouthful she has; she is sucking it, just as you are sucking mine. How nice it feels to have one's prick sucked. Oh! Nelly, I can't go on, let it out, it's just coming," and he tried to draw it away, but I was enjoying so much the taste of his prick in my mouth, and, at the same time, had such a wonderful feel in my cunt that I would not let it go, so holding the cheeks of his bottom I moved him backward and forward, and made him fuck me in my mouth. His prick swelled, I felt it throb, and then a hot stream of sperm spurted into my mouth and flowed down my throat. We soon heard Uncle leaving Lizzy's room, then Gussy went too and all was quiet.

Uncle went to her room nearly every night, and though, during the day they were most particular in their conduct towards each other, and she, with her large blue eyes, looked the very picture of innocence, yet at night they gave themselves up to the most unbounded license. He fucked her in every conceivable attitude and way. He made her use every amorous term, even words that are generally thought vulgar and coarse. He used to lie on the rug before the fire on his back, when she, all naked would straddle over him, and with her cunt resting on his mouth, would stoop down and suck his prick. Then, when she had it standing up stiff and strong, she would place its head between the lips of her cunt, and sitting down would force it up. Then he would place his hands under her bottom, and help her to rise up and down. At other times he would lean back in the armchair, and she would sit in his lap, her naked bottom rubbing against his belly, while his prick was soaking in her cunt, and her hands on his balls.

I heard her say she liked this plan best, as his prick seemed to get further into her cunt.

Gussy and I watched them with the greatest interest, as long as my visit lasted, and tried to follow them in their various evolutions, frigging, sucking, fucking.

Holding the chamber pot for each other to make water; and every possible idea we could think of to vary the fun.

AN EPISTLE TO A LADY.

Mrs. T. T., wife of a lawyer; she had first been the wife of Dr. F., another lawyer.

Some moments in life, I could wish very long,
Because as the monkey said, pleasant but wrong;
'Tis sweet to remember some frolics I've had,
Though the angel who suffered them cries out, "Too bad."
Yes, grant me that angel, another man's wife,
She is by law, but to me she is life;
That rich feast of pleasure, that rapture, I'd call it,
That devil that tickles my intellect's palate.
I'm well read in woman, I seldom can find,
One that brings a new relish of joy to my mind;
But she's quite a treat, one that never can pall,
Think all you can think, she surpasses it all.
Oh would that I had her! -and had her just now,
I can make love much better, than verses, I vow;
Her, I ardently covet, and love, and esteem,
I saw but last night, in a sweet Golden Dream.
The dress that she wore, fitted close as her skin,
'Twas of Paradise fashion, ere fig leaves came in;
Her smooth birthday suit, all of flesh colour'd buff,
With a furbelow too, a divine little muff.
But a creature so fair's a mere victim for evil,
So she straightway received an address from the devil;

He came drest like a lawyer, so grand and severe,
And assured her she suited him, just to a hair.
O how could she bear such a lifeless old lover,
She who palpitates warm with excitement all over;
She who throbs like my heart, on the ravishing stretch,
How could she endure such a cold-blooded wretch?
She smiled at his pleadings - and then she saw me.
It was just before tasting the wit-giving tree!
And the barrister prim, a great man in his college,
Was to introduce her to the fair tree of knowledge.
But alas; with that knowledge, came misery too,
And the Eve of my vision, evanished from view;
The devil soon died, but the very next glimpse,
Betrayed she had now married one of his imps!
To escape the dull phiz of this crabbed attorney,
She to Italy flew, on a classical journey;
Next I met her, more lovely, though after young years,
In her dear little parlour, so private, up-stairs.
There knee pressing knee, and kind eyes within eyes,
Our converse still broken, with fluttering sighs;
We talked about books, and the way to improve,
But our tremors confessed the sweet fever of love.
Ah! would that we both had had wisdom at will,
Though it might have prevented us kissing our fill!
Those blisses are short, that most heavenly seem,
I woke, and behold, it was merely a dream!

LADY POKINGHAM, OR THEY ALL DO IT

Giving an Account of her Luxurious Adventures, both before and after her Marriage with Lord Crim-Con

*

Part III

(Continued.)

Alice led me by the hand, having closed the door behind us; a cold shiver passed over my frame, but plucking up courage, I never faltered, and we soon found a little green baize door, bolted on our side. "Hush!" she said, "this opens into quite a dark corner, behind the confessional box," as she gently withdrew the bolt, and we then noiselessly entered the chapel into a little kind of passage, between the box and the wall, and fortunately protected from observation by a large open-work screen, which completely hid us, but afforded quite a good view of the interior of the chapel. Guess our astonishment when we beheld both Lady St. Jerome and her niece in earnest conference with the two priests and overheard what passed.

FATHER COLEMAN. - "Well, Sister Clare, the Cardinal has ordered that you are to seduce Lothair, by all the arts in your power; every venial sin you may commit is already forgiven."

MONSIGNORE, addressing Lady St. Jerome. - "Yes, and Sister Agatha here will assist you all she can; you know she is a nun, but by the modern policy of Holy Church, we allow certain of the sisters to marry when their union with influential men tends to further the interests of the Church; the secret sisterhood of St. Bridget is one of the most powerful political institutions in the world, because unsuspected, and its members have all sworn to obey with both body and soul; in fact, Sister Clare, this holy sisterhood into which we have just admitted you, by this special faculty from his Eminence, will permit you to enjoy every possible sensual pleasure here upon earth, and insure your heavenly reward as well."

The bright light shows us plainly the blushing face of Clare Arundel, which is turned almost crimson, as the confessor whispers something to her. "Ah! No! No! No! not now," she cried out.

MONSIGNORE. - "The first act of sisterhood is always to do penance directly after admission, and you have taken the oaths to obey both in body and mind, sister Agatha will blindfold you, throw off your robe, and submit your body to the mortification of the flesh."

Lady St. Jerome quickly removed the dressing-gown in which her niece was enveloped, and left the fair girl with nothing but her chemise to cover her beautiful figure; the bandage was speedily adjusted over her lovely eyes, and she was made to kneel on a cushion, and rest her arms and face on the rails of the altar. Father Coleman armed himself with a light scourge of small cords, fixed in a handle, whilst her ladyship turned up the chemise of the victim so as to expose her bottom, thighs, legs and back to his castigation; then she withdrew, and seated herself on the knee of Monsignore, who had made himself comfortable in a large chair close to the victim; he clasped her round the waist, and pressed his lips to hers, whilst their hands seemed to indulge in a mutual groping about each other's private parts.

The scourge fell upon the lovely bottom; each stroke drawing a painful sigh from the victim, and leaving long red weals on the tender flesh.

The confessor continually lectured her on her future duties, and made her promise to do all his commands.

The poor girl's bottom was soon scored all over, and dripping with blood; the sight of which seemed to inflame the others, so that the confessor's affair stood out between the opening of his cassock, whilst Lady St. Jerome spitted herself on the pego of Monsignore, and rode a most gallant St. George as he sat in the chair.

THE CONFESSOR. - "Now, sister, for the last mortification of your flesh, you must surrender your virginity to the Church." Saying which, he produced several fine large cushions, took the bandage from her eyes, and laid her comfortably on her back for his attack, with an extra cushion under her buttocks, in the most approved fashion. Then kneeling down between her thighs, he opened his cassock, and we could see he was almost naked underneath. He laid himself forward on her lovely body, and whispered something in her ear, which was apparently a command to her to take hold of his lustful weapon, for she immediately put down her hand, and seemed (as far as we could see) to direct it to her crack herself. She was evidently fired with lust, and longing to allay the raging heat of the part which had been so cruelly whipped, for she heaved up her bottom to meet his attack, and so seconded his efforts that he speedily forced his way in, and the only evidence of pain on her part was a rather sharp little cry, just as he entered to break through the hymen. They lay for a moment in the enjoyment of the loving conjunction of their parts; but she was impatient, putting her hands on the cheeks of his bottom, and pressing him to herself in a most lascivious manner, and just then Monsignore and Sister Agatha, who had finished their course, got up, and one with the scourge, and the other with a thin cane (after first lifting up his cassock and exposing a brown hairy-looking bottom), began to lay on to Father Coleman in good earnest. Thus stimulated, and begging and crying for them to let him alone, he rammed furiously into Miss Clare, to her evident delight; she wriggled, writhed, and screamed in ecstasy, and gave us such a sight of sensual delirium as I have never seen before or since. At last he seemed to spend into her, and, after a while, withdrew himself from her reluctant embrace, as she seemed to try hard to get him to go on again.

We could see they were preparing to leave the chapel, so thought it time to make our retreat.

Next day we were presented, and nothing in the manner of the lively Lady St. Jerome, or the demure Miss Clare Arundel, would have led anyone to imagine the scene that we had witnessed in the small hours of the morning.

In the evening we were all at the Duchess's ball. Lord Carisbrooke, to whom I was specially introduced, was my partner in the set, in which danced Lothair and Miss Arundel as vis-a-vis to

Lady Corisande and the Duke of Brecon.

Bye-and-bye the hero of the evening led me out for the Lancers, and afterwards we strolled into the conservatory, quite unobserved; his conversation was much livelier than I had expected, for Lady St. Jerome had represented to us that he was seriously bent on religion, and about to join the Romish Church. The conservatory was large, and we strolled on till the music and laughter seemed quite at a distance, and coming to a seat with a delightful fountain in front of us we sat down, but just as he was observing, "How delightful it was to withdraw from the whirl of gaiety for a few minutes," we heard some light footsteps approaching, and evidently a very loving couple, the lady exclaiming, with a saucy laugh, "Ah! No! How dare you presume so; I would never be unfaithful to Montairy even in a kiss"; there was a slight struggle, and, "Ah, Monster, what a liberty!" and we heard the smack of lips upon a soft cheek, and then, "Oh! No! Let me go back," but the gentleman evidently remonstrated, as I could hear him say, "Come, come, compose yourself, dear Victoria, a little, there is a seat here by the fountain, you must rest a moment,"

Lothair, with a start, whispered - "They must not catch us here, they'd think we had been eavesdropping; let's hide ourselves and never say a word about it," dragging me by the hand around a corner, where we were well screened by the foliage of the delicious exotics.

My heart was in a flutter, and I could perceive he was greatly moved. We stood motionless, hand in hand, as the lady and gentleman took possession of the cool seat we had just vacated; the latter proved to be the Duke of Brecon. I could see them plainly, and have no doubt Lothair did also.

LADY MONTAIRY. - "Now, sir, no more of your impudent pranks. Pray let me recover my serenity."

The Duke knelt down and took her hand, which she affectedly tried to withdraw, but he retained it, saying:

"Dearest Victoria, pity my passion. How can I help loving those killing eyes, and luscious pouting lips. That very fact of its being wrong makes my determination the greater to enjoy you the first opportunity. It is useless to resist our fate: Why has the God of Love given me such a chance as this?"

She turns away her head with affected prudery; but not a blush rises to assert her horror at his speech. One hand presses her fingers to his lips; but where is the other? Under her clothes. He first touches her ankle, and slowly steals it up her leg. She fidgets on the seat, but he is impetuous, and soon has possession of her most secret charms. Her languishing eyes are turned on him, and in an instant, he is on his legs, and pushing her clothes up, displays a lovely pair of legs in white silk stockings, beautiful blue garters with gold buckles, her thighs encased in rather tight-fitting drawers, beautifully trimmed with Valenciennes lace. His lips are glued to hers at the same instant, and his hands gently part her yielding thighs, as he placed himself well between them. It is but the work of an instant. He places her hand on the shaft of love, which he has just let out, and it is guided into the haven of love. Both are evidently too hot and impetuous, for it seems to be over in a minute.

She hastily kisses him, and puts down her clothes as she says: "How awful; but I could not resist Your Grace without disordering all my dress. It's been quite a rape, sir," with a smile. "Now, let's make haste back before we are missed." He kisses her, and makes her agree to an assignation, somewhere in South Belgravia, for the morrow, to enjoy each other more at leisure, and then they were gone.

It would be impossible to describe the agitation of my partner during this short scene; Lothair seemed to shiver and shudder with emotion, I was also all of a tremble, and nestled close to him, my arm designedly touching the bunch in his trousers, always so interesting to me; I could feel it swell and seem ready to burst from its confinement; he nervously clasped my hand, and was speechless with emotion all during the scene which I have described; as soon as they were gone he seemed to give a gasp of relief, and led me out of our hiding place. "Poor girl," he said, "what a sight for you, how I trembled for my own honour, lest the scene should make me lose my self-control. Ah! wretched woman, to betray your husband so!" Then looking at me for the first time he said, "Do you not think it is best for a man never to marry?"

Used as I had been to such things, his terrible emotion made me quite sympathize with him, and my own agitation was quite natural, as I replied, "Ah! my Lord, you little know the ways of the world; I saw a more awful scene than what we have witnessed, only last night, enacted by men sworn to perpetual celibacy, and you yourself were mentioned as a victim to their infernal plot."

"My God! Lady, pray tell me what it was," he ejaculated.

"Not now, we shall be missed, do you know any place where I can have a private conference with your lordship? If so, meet me tomorrow afternoon at two o'clock, in the Burlington Arcade. I shall come disguised," I answered.

(To be continued.)

MAKING BACON

A Jew who wanted to get hold of a Miss Bacon, said:
If I took but a slice,
Of pig's flesh, so nice,
Our rabbis would bluster and take on.
But I'd brave all their damns,
For a touch at the hams,
Of this delicate red and white Bacon.

DIVERSION

When Molly the housemaid, who lived at the "Blue Boar," at York, was married to John the Ostler, her mistress gave the poor couple a bedchamber, in a garret, to celebrate their nuptials. But Robert and Harry, who had long well known all Poor Molly's in and outs, were seriously anxious to know the result. They crept to the door, and at last heard Molly exclaim: "Ah! Johnny dearest, you are where man never was before!"

"Zounds, Harry!" whispered Robert; "he must have got into her arse."

SONG

How lovely did Venus at first seem to be,
When her birth she received from the spring of the sea;
As red as a rose looked her cunt's lovely rim,
And the foam slowly dripped from the hairs of her quim!
Her belly was whiter than marble, I ween,
And above it her bubbies like snow balls were seen;
But Venus was still discontented, alas,
She wanted a prick and two balls at her arse!

Her thighs were so pure, so graceful and round,
None fairer and lovelier e'er could be found;
But her cunt, I dare say, great pleasure it sips,
With a stiff-standing penis to part its red lips!
Oh, poking is a pleasure, we all must enjoy.
Tho' I had it for ever, it never would cloy;
To any young man on the grass I would fall.
And if cunt would allow it, take bollox and all!

THE REVERIE

What dull and senseless lumps we'd be,
If never of felicity
We tasted; and what bliss is there
To equal that of fucking rare?
An age of grief, an age of pain,
I would endure and ne'er complain;
To purchase but an hour's charms,
While wriggling in a maiden's arms!

And hugging her to heavenly rest,
My hand reposing on her breast!
Her arse my own, her thighs my screen.
My penis standing in between!
My bollox hanging down below.
And banging 'gainst her arse of snow;
Or else grasped firmly in her hand,
To make my yard more stiffly stand.

How soon the blood glows in the veins,
And nature all its power now strains;
The belly heaves, the penis burns.
The maiden all its heat returns,
Till passion holds triumphant sway.
And both the lovers die away.

A MAIDEN'S WISH.

When wishes first enter a maiden's breast.
She longs by her lover to be carest;
She longs with her lover to do the trick,
And in secret she longs for a taste of his prick!
Her cunt it is itching from morning till night,
The prick of her lover can yield her delight;
She longs to be fucked, and for that does deplore,
For what can a young maiden wish for more?
If fever or sickness her spirits doth shock,
Why, we know what she wants, 'tis a stiff-standing cock!

Give her a prick, it will soon make her well,
Though perhaps in the long run, her belly may swell!
She'd like very well to be laid on the grass.
To have two ample bollox sent bang 'gainst her arse;
She longs to be fucked, and for that does deplore,
For what can a young maiden wish for more?
It's a pity any quim hungry should go,
All maids wish them filled, as you very well know,
And if the young men would be ready and free,
They'd up with their clouts in a trice, d'ye see!

She wants to be ask'd, but to ask is afraid,
And fearful she is that she'll die an old maid;
She wishes for prick, and for that does deplore,
For what can a young maiden wish for more?

THE JOYS OF COMING TOGETHER

Tell me where are there such blisses
As the sexes can impart?
When lips join in heavenly kisses,
When they both convulsive start!
Throbbing, heaving,
Never grieving;
Thrusting, bursting,
Sighing, dying!
All nature now is in aglow,
Now they're coming, oh! oh!! oh!!!
Mutual keeping to one tether.
Sweet it is to come together!
Decrepit age is only teasing.
Shrivelled-up pricks, who can abide?
Vigorous youth, oh, that is pleasing,
It is worth the world beside!
Craving, wanting,
Sobbing, panting,
Throbbing, heaving,
Never grieving,
Thrusting, bursting,
Sighing, dying!
All nature now is in a glow,
Now they're coming, oh! oh!! oh!!!
Mutual keeping to one tether,
Sweet it is to come together.

NURSERY RHYMES.

A parson who lived near Cremorne
Looked down on all women with scorn;
E'en a boy's white fat bum;
Could not make him come;
But an old man's piles gave him the horn.

A cheerful old party of Lucknow,
Remarked, "I should like a fuck now!"
So he had one and spent,
And said, "I'm content!
By no means am I so cunt-struck now."

There was a young man of Peru,
Who lived upon clap juice and spew;
When these palled to his taste,
He tried some turd paste,
And said that was very good too.

There is a new Baron of Wokingham;
The girls say he don't care for poking 'em.
Preferring "Minette,"
What is pleasant, but ye,
There is one disadvantage, his choking 'em.

There was an Archbishop of Rheims,

Who played with himself in his dreams;
On his nightshirt in front,
He painted a cunt,
Which made his spend gush forth in streams.

There was a young man of Newminster Court.
Bugger'd a pig, but his prick was too snort;
Said the hog, "It's not nice;
But pray take my advice;
Make tracks, or by the police you'll be caught."

There was a young man of Cashmere.
Who purchased a fine Bayadere!
He fucked all her toes.
Her mouth, eyes, and her nose,
And eventually poxed her left ear.

There was a young party of Bicester,
Who wanted to bugger his sister;
But not liking dirt.
He bought him a squirt,
And cleaned out her arse with a clyster.

There was a young man of King's Cross,
Who amused himself frigging a horse.
Then licking the spend
Which still dripped from the end,
Said, "It tastes just like anchovy sauce."

A president called Gambetta.
Once used an imperfect French Letter;
This was not the worst,
With disease he got cursed.
And he took a long time to get better.

There was a young girl from Vistula,
To whom a friend said, "Jef has kissed you, la!"
Said she, "Yes, by God!

But my arse he can't sod,
Because I am troubled with Fistula."

AFTER-THOUGHT

A new patent shoe-horn, for the insertions of big pricks into tight bum-holes, is reported to have been invented by a lady member of the Comedie Francaise, who is said to place the half skin of a peach, turned inside out, upon the tip of a lover's penis, before he is allowed to enculer his chere amie, who prefers bum-fucking to the old orthodox plan of coition.

"I see you have your everlasting stocking on," said her fond papa, at Southend, to a Whitechapel young lady, who was wading bare-legged on the beach. "I don't know about that, father, for my arse is covered with the same stuff, and that's got a hole in it."

Made in the USA
Coppell, TX
26 March 2024

30555971R00111